GLOBAL URBAN SPACES

From the pre-Islamic Jahilia, early modern Sikri and Florence, to postcolonial Bombay and Karachi, cities have played a pivotal role in Salman Rushdie's fiction. This book focuses on spatial concerns and urban imaginaries in his works, challenging the dominant metropolitan discourse on cities under globalization.

Rushdie's works prominently feature cities of the Global South while they explore the figure of the postcolonial migrant in great detail. This book examines the evolving portrayal of cities in selected novels, from *Midnight's Children* (1981) to *Victory City* (2023), and explores the concept of the global-urban. It examines how these works explore alternative geo-histories, the idea of global homes, and the idea of cities as sites of conflict and contestation, where histories and memories are embedded and reimagined.

This book will be useful for scholars and researchers of literature, urban studies, cultural studies, postcolonial studies, sociology, Indian English, and South Asian literature.

Madhumita Roy is currently serving as an Assistant Professor in the Department of Humanities and Social Sciences at the Indian Institute of Engineering Science and Technology (IIEST), Shibpur, India. She has published extensively in these areas in reputed peer-reviewed journals, including *The Journal of Commonwealth Literature*, *GeoHumanities*, *The Journal of Urban Cultural Studies*, *Dialogues in Human Geography*, *Balkanistic Forum*, and *Cosmopolitan Civil Societies*, among others.

Anjali Gera Roy is a former Professor in the Department of Humanities and Social Sciences at IIT Kharagpur, where she taught courses in language, literature, and communication for over 35 years. Her research spans linguistic, literary, cultural, and performing traditions of India, along with oral histories, folklore, postcolonial, and diaspora studies. Her recent publications include *Regional Perspectives on India's Partition: Shifting the Vantage Points* (with Nandi Bhatia, 2023), *Memories and Postmemories of the Partition of India* (2019), and *Cinema of Enchantment: Perso-Arabic Genealogies of the Hindi Masala Film* (2015).

GLOBAL URBAN SPACES

Reimagining the City in Salman Rushdie's Novels

Madhumita Roy and Anjali Gera Roy

Routledge
Taylor & Francis Group

LONDON AND NEW YORK

Designed cover image: Getty Images

First published 2026
by Routledge
4 Park Square, Milton Park, Abingdon, Oxon OX14 4RN

and by Routledge
605 Third Avenue, New York, NY 10158

Routledge is an imprint of the Taylor & Francis Group, an informa business

© 2026 Madhumita Roy and Anjali Gera Roy

British Library Cataloguing-in-Publication Data
A catalogue record for this book is available from the British Library

ISBN: 978-0-367-54135-4 (hbk)
ISBN: 978-0-367-61718-9 (pbk)
ISBN: 978-1-003-10618-0 (ebk)

DOI: 10.4324/9781003106180

Typeset in Sabon
by Deanta Global Publishing Services, Chennai, India

CONTENTS

PREFACE

This book, *Global Urban Spaces: Reimagining the City in Salman Rushdie's Novels*, is a revised form of a thesis that was originally submitted by Madhumita Roy to the Department of Humanities and Social Sciences, IIT Kharagpur, under the supervision of Prof. Anjali Gera Roy. The journey from thesis to manuscript has been long and, at times, fraught with personal and professional challenges. Nevertheless, we are grateful for the unwavering support of the editors and stood by us, ensuring that this work would ultimately find its way to publication.

The central theme of this book—urban space in a globalized world—has become increasingly urgent in our time. Global cities today stand at a paradoxical crossroads: while they operate as key nodes in the circuits of transnational capital, innovation, and commerce, they are simultaneously the sites where the human costs of globalization become most visible. These urban centres, celebrated as engines of economic growth and cultural convergence, are also the very spaces where international migration, displacement, and precarity are most acutely experienced. As people move across borders—driven by war, climate change, political instability, and economic need—cities become zones of contestation as much as of opportunity. They embody both the promise of cosmopolitan futures and the inequalities embedded in global systems. In this context, the novels of Salman Rushdie offer a particularly incisive lens through which to examine the layered dynamics of urban life. His cities are more than mere settings—they are palimpsests of memory, violence, myth, and movement, capturing the contradictions at the heart of the global urban experience.

We would like to take this opportunity to express our sincere gratitude to everyone who supported this project along the way. Our families, for their patience and encouragement, have been our strongest pillars throughout this journey. A special word of thanks is due to Prof. Anjali Gera Roy—not only for her invaluable guidance during the initial stages of this research at IIT Kharagpur but also for her continued collaboration as co-author of this book. We also thank Soham Mukherjee, a PhD scholar at IIEST Shibpur, for his editorial assistance during the final stages of manuscript preparation. Parts of this book were previously published in revised forms in the following journals, and we gratefully acknowledge their editors and publishers for the permission to reproduce and further develop those ideas here: *Journal of Urban Cultural Studies, Glocalism: A Journal of Culture, Politics and Innovation,* and *GeoHumanities.* These platforms provided early avenues for exploring key arguments that have since been expanded and contextualized within this manuscript.

We hope this book serves as a meaningful contribution to the ongoing discussions surrounding global urban spaces, migration, and the complex realities of postcolonial cities as reflected in the work of Salman Rushdie.

1

INTRODUCTION

The 2022 attack on Salman Rushdie during a public event in Chautauqua, New York, is a stark reminder of the dangers writers face when their work challenges boundaries. This incident brings to mind the "Rushdie Affair" of 1989, after the release of *The Satanic Verses* (1988). The novel's exploration of faith, identity, and religion led to a *fatwa* calling for Rushdie's death by Ayatollah Ruhollah Khomeini, the Supreme Leader of Iran. What makes the recent attack even more striking is that it took place in a global, cosmopolitan city. Rushdie, as a public intellectual, was in a space meant to be secure for open discourse, yet he faced similar tensions linked to extremism that have shaped global geopolitics since the 1980s. The fact that the attacker was 24, born a few years after *The Satanic Verses* was published, shows how the controversies around Rushdie's work continue to take on new significance. Though Rushdie has written an autobiographical book reflecting on the attack—*Knife: Meditations After an Attempted Murder* (2024)—his earlier works still stand as a testament to the ongoing relevance of the issues that sparked it. The radicalism that once took root in Iran and Lebanon (where the attacker's family is from) continues to echo in places like New York, a city shaped by forces from distant places and times, which also highlights the need to view Rushdie's writings in the broader context of global cities and the complex forces that shape them.

Rushdie, born in Bombay in 1947, has spent much of his life in the bustling metropolitan centres of the world. Leaving Bombay for London at the age of fourteen, he has since lived in cities such as New York, London, Karachi, Florence, and Los Angeles, each playing a significant role in his personal life and literary work. As a writer, Rushdie's connection to urban

DOI: 10.4324/9781003106180-1

spaces is evident, with his novels frequently centred in vibrant, dynamic cities. Cities like Bombay, Karachi, London, New York, and Los Angeles have been crucial to the development of his fiction, yet their importance has often been overlooked in critical analysis—until recently. Although some literary studies have examined the role of cities in Rushdie's work and their connection to broader questions regarding the contemporary urban condition, these studies have largely overlooked the new interdisciplinary insights from emerging research on cities. This book aims to address this gap by examining Rushdie's novels through the lens of cities as "social spaces," drawing on Henri Lefebvre's seminal work on spatial theory (1991). The study will focus on novels such as *Midnight's Children* (1981), *Shame* (1983), *The Satanic Verses* (1988), *The Moor's Last Sigh* (1995), *The Ground Beneath Her Feet* (1999), *Fury* (2001), *Shalimar the Clown* (2005), *The Enchantress of Florence* (2008), *Two Years Eight Months and Twenty-Eight Nights* (2015), *The Golden House* (2017), *Quichotte* (2019), and *Victory City* (2023). By adopting an interdisciplinary approach, this book seeks to engage with the growing discourse on global cities, those identified as "strategic territories" by Saskia Sassen (1991), and proposes an alternative understanding of global urban spaces as portrayed in Rushdie's novels. This study aims to rethink the concept of the global city in two key ways: first, by applying Edward Soja's concept of synekism to global cities, offering a diachronic perspective on globalization; and second, by critiquing the urban conditions in both the Global South and the Global North through the complex, multi-scalar movements of the postcolonial migrant in Rushdie's fiction.

Cities have long been central to epics, romances, and poetry as settings, but the novel and the everyday urban experience are deeply interconnected in more ways than one. As Ian Watt (1957) notes in his influential study, the rise of the novel is tied to realism in the arts, which demands engagement with specific time and place, as opposed to the mythic and ritualistic time and space of epics and romances. The eighteenth century, a period defined by the Industrial Revolution and the Enlightenment, marked the emergence of the novel as a literary form, coinciding with the rise of the modern city. It is unsurprising that many iconic novelists throughout history have been seen as chroniclers of urban life. Yet, their approaches to the depiction of city vary widely. Two such influential figures, Charles Dickens and James Joyce, had a profound effect on Rushdie. Dickens, known for his combination of journalistic detail and surrealism, provides both an accurate and melodramatic, caricatured portrayal of nineteenth-century London during the height of the British Empire and the Industrial Revolution. His works capture the energy of London life, weaving theatrical, fairy-tale-like characters into the gritty, realistic fabric of the city. In contrast, Joyce's portrayal of Dublin in *Ulysses* (1922) adopts a different literary technique: stream of consciousness. His Dublin, much like Dickens's London, becomes a place where the mythical coexists with the real. Joyce's Dublin carries an air of despair and bleakness, highlighting the crisis of modernity in the metropolis. Rushdie's relationship with realism, much like that of Dickens and Joyce, is complex. His use of magical realism and the blending of the mythical with the real have been explained through his eclectic influences—from Eastern (Hindu and Muslim) narrative traditions to Western postmodernism. In his works, cities become spaces where the mythical and the real coexist in equal measure, mirroring the urban landscapes of Dickens and Joyce, resulting in playful interconnections with the "other" spaces. Rushdie's real-imagined cities provide a lens through which we can explore multiple "invisible cities" within the visible city, enriching our understanding of both the crisis and regenerative potential of the contemporary urban experience. These cities, much like the ones in Joyce and Dickens, offer opportunities for exploring the complex intersections of reality and imagination.

Rushdie's urban landscapes lead to two primary insights in this book: the cities in his novels are both "social" and "lived," and they are "global" urban spaces. The concepts of "social" and "lived" space are derived from Henri Lefebvre's groundbreaking work *The Production of Space* (1991). Lefebvre argued that space is not a passive setting but a product shaped by human interaction. His spatial triad—conceived space (representations of space), perceived space (spatial practice), and lived space (representational spaces)—emphasizes the importance of lived space, or the space of the "users" and "inhabitants," which contrasts with abstract or material perspectives on space. The cities in Rushdie's novels, being both imaginary and real, can be seen as social space, with their lived spaces documenting the experiences of people who engage with symbols and myths from other times and places. The idea of "global" urban space is more flexible in its application. In Rushdie's novels, cities are sites of interconnections that transcend geographical boundaries. These interconnections create what can be termed "global" spaces, not just in the context of late twentieth and early twenty-first-century globalization but as an ongoing process since historical times. Historians, archaeologists, and sociologists suggest that globalization has always existed to some extent, and its traces are visible in the cities Rushdie portrays. These cities are shaped not only by connections to the past but also by complex, non-hierarchical interactions between cities in the Global North and South, which challenge the normative views in contemporary globalization studies. This dynamic contributes to a continuous process of "rethinking" global space in Rushdie's works. In the following sections, we will explore the connections between key concepts that are essential for understanding the process of "rethinking."

Globalization, Postcolonialism, and the End of the Nation-State

The concept of globalization has gained substantial attention across various fields, including literary and cultural studies, geography, economics, and other social sciences, over the past few decades. Keywords like "borderless world," "global village," "deterritorialization," "flows," and "transnationalism" are frequently used in contemporary discourse. Globalization refers to the interconnected movement of people, ideas, and capital that surpasses national borders, significantly shaping the modern world. However, many critics of globalization challenge the view that contemporary globalization is a phenomenon unique to the Global North. They argue for alternative, non-Eurocentric narratives that acknowledge the distinctive forms of modernity in the Global South. Some scholars further emphasize that globalization is not a recent phenomenon but rather a long-standing, historical process that predates European colonialism, highlighting global interconnectedness outside European mediation. While materialist critics view globalization as a byproduct of capitalist machinery and postmodernity, others stress its non-materialistic aspects, such as the development of "global consciousness" (Robertson, 1992).

Postcolonialism, as a critical response to European colonial expansion, addresses how imperial legacies continue to affect both the former colonies and their former colonizers in the globalized world. Many postcolonial scholars, including Gayatri Spivak and Homi Bhabha, grapple with how globalization reshapes the postcolonial world, deconstructing the binaries of colonizer and colonized while both critiquing and embracing a "hybrid" globalized existence. Spivak (2013), for instance, promotes an aesthetic education that cultivates an awareness of how the global subjects navigate complex ethical and political terrains, without compromising their identities while critiquing the pervasive imperialism of global capital, which has affected even institutions like US universities, where neoliberal values dominate. Similarly, Homi Bhabha (2010) underscores the power of literature and art as forms of resistance to global capital's dominance, challenging the efficacy of traditional political movements in confronting the forces of inequality.

In both postcolonial and globalization studies, particularly those working in the context of international relations, the nation-state forms the basis of the dualistic model of the centre and the periphery. Benedict Anderson's (1983) influential concept of the nation as an "imagined community," defined by its limits and sovereignty, provides a powerful lens through which to explore the ideological dimensions of nationalism, contrasting with the materialist, repressive mechanisms of state power. According to Anderson, the nation-state is a product of European modernity and industrial capitalism. The nation-state also serves as the most essential political unit in the narrative of the colonial struggle for the once colonized third-world. Colonial struggles were once fought for the autonomy of respective (perhaps contingent) national cultures, but the formation of the postcolonial nation-state has been a historically arbitrary process. The geopolitical borders of the nation-state were sometimes carved out randomly by colonizers creating representational spaces promoted by the ocular views of colonizers, and pseudo-scientific discourses of cartography and geography promoting the imperialist agendas of colonial modernity. A prime example would be the division of India and Pakistan on the eve of India's independence on 15 August 1947, which appears in Rushdie's *Midnight's Children*. A defaulter since its birth, many postcolonial nation-states have also been accused of failing their citizens on multiple registers—promoting dictatorship, sham democracies, elite representational democracies, state-sponsored ethnic riots, genocides, corrupt and criminalized state machineries, majoritarianism, etc. As Ranajit Guha (1982) points out, India as a postcolonial nation-state served the interest of the elite rather than the subaltern who, as Gayatri Spivak (1988) claims, cannot speak out, not only in the face of colonial violence but also in the supposedly egalitarian registers of the postcolonial nation-state. National cultures also turned militant in a hastily globalizing world that Edward Said (1993) compares to the atavistic impulses of the tribalizing latent within the modernity of the nation-state.

The relationship between globalization and the nation-state has been the subject of significant debate. Many argue that globalization weakens the nation-state, particularly in economic, political, and cultural realms, due to the formation of networks that surpass national boundaries—such as multinational corporations, global terrorism, and environmental issues. David Held (2000) believes that the nation-state is an inadequate unit to explain the conditions and requirements of the present world that may be explained through "overlapping communities of fate," which transcend the geopolitical borders of the nation-states. Held further proposes that the globalized world requires an evolved form of "cosmopolitan" principles based on equality in worth, dignity, accountability, consent, etc., which might develop an alternative form of cultural, economic, political, and legal frameworks to state sovereignty. Thus, Held considers the process of globalization intricately linked to the values of cosmopolitanism which, since the Greek Stoics in antiquity and Kant's revolutionary ideas of Enlightenment, have advocated human beings' affiliation to the world over their immediate locality. Jurgen Habermas (Held and McGrew, 2000) offers a more cautious perspective, arguing that global governance should not completely disregard national perspectives, as national identities still matter for addressing inequalities. Habermas also advancing the empowering legacies of Enlightenment posits a sceptical view of cosmopolitan frameworks that are destabilizing the sovereignty of the nation-state in the contemporary world. According to Habermas, the global order lacks ethico-political dimensions that might lead to transnational will formations to address the massive socio-economic inequalities of our times, which, perhaps, might be achieved in the form of "global governance" emerging from, instead of excluding, national perspectives. Fredric Jameson (1986) provides a nuanced view by claiming that, although globalization has created a "postmodern hyperspace," the nation-state remains relevant in the third-world, where it still serves as a site of resistance. The nation-sate and the national culture retain their political agency in the third-world as Jameson reads all third-world literatures, even in the age of late capitalism, as national allegories (1986). In contrast, Bill Ashcroft envisions the "transnation" as a potential way to liberate from the oppressive power of the nation-state. Ashcroft believes in the utopia of the transnation, which, according to him, has the potential of amending the narrow parameters and oppressions of the postcolonial nation-state. Ashcroft says "What if the transnational does not begin when national borders are crossed, but already exists within nations themselves? What if the transnational begins by crossing internal boundaries?" (2017: 47). He believes that the term "transnation" is proposed to describe the movement of people within, and occasionally across, national borders, where their circulation around state boundaries reduces the nation's role in shaping their identity. This shift reflects a broader global trend where stable relations of dominance and subordination are replaced by instability, insecurity, and deprivation, as seen in the rise of refugees and asylum seekers. However, the focus should not just be on the movement of people across borders but on the deeper destabilization of state power, particularly in cities. According to him, the postcolonial city exemplifies how urban areas have become focal points for transnational movements, marking a historical shift in the role of cities within this global dynamic (2017).

However, for a more complex understanding of contemporary globalization, Arjun Appadurai (1996) introduces the concept of "scapes"—five dimensions that explain the dynamic flows of globalization: ethnoscapes, mediascapes, technoscapes, financescapes, and ideoscapes. These "scapes" represent a fluid, interconnected global cultural economy that transcends traditional territorial boundaries, offering a platform for subverting dominant narratives. Appadurai's work reflects the decentralization of power in the global age. Transnational communities, which are more mobile and less bound by territorial affiliations, have become vital agents in these fluid spaces. These communities offer empowering possibilities by providing more egalitarian forms of participation and belonging. However, the process of globalization also has its contradictions. On the one hand, it undermines the nation-state's power, while on the other, it exacerbates the crisis of capitalism, producing inequality and alienation within globalized spaces. In this sense, globalization's "smooth space" presents both an opportunity for liberation and a site of continued crisis, as traditional state-based structures are insufficient to address the challenges of late capitalism.

Thus, globalization is reshaping the postcolonial world, influencing both the cultural and political landscape. While the nation-state's role is increasingly questioned, it continues to shape global power relations, prompting new critical perspectives on how we understand and navigate the complexities of the modern, interconnected world. Through this framework, scholars can better engage with contemporary issues, examining the interplay between global flows and localized experiences in the age of globalization.

The Spatial Turn and the City

The concept of "space" has gained significant attention in globalization theories due to the rapidly shrinking world. The dynamics of contemporary globalization raise important questions about the status of place in a world characterized by flows, networks, and interconnectedness. This globalized world underscores the critical issues surrounding the production of space, confronting the crisis in spatial production while also highlighting new ways of strategically creating space. In light of the decline of the nation-state in a deterritorialized world, there has been a rise of the city as an alternative spatial scale, playing a crucial role in reterritorializing global flows. This shift marks a departure from traditional Western thinking, which typically regarded space as a passive backdrop, while time was seen as the active force driving change. Reclaiming space and place as active agents of social transformation is not just a social issue but also an ontological and epistemological one. The importance of space in relation to social existence is evident in Martin Heidegger's idea of *Dasein*, where human beings are fundamentally "emplaced." In a similar vein, Fredric Jameson (1991) emphasizes the significance of "cognitive mapping" in his "political form of postmodernism," where individuals, whose subjectivity has been dominated by capitalism, can regain their creative abilities and power to act. The notion that human beings are "situated beings-in-the-world" underscores the idea that our creativity and ability to engage with the world are closely tied to the spaces we inhabit.

Foucault, in his essay "Of Other Spaces" (1986), reflects on the change in our experience of the world, noting that our perception is less shaped by the passage of time and more by a network of interconnected points. He says:

> We are at a moment, I believe, when our experience of the world is less that of a long life developing through time than that of a network that connects points and intersects with its own skein.
>
> *(Foucault, 1986: 22)*

For Foucault, it is "space, not time, that hides consequences from us," and he foresaw that the present epoch would be dominated by space. This shift towards understanding space as an active force has led to the "spatial turn" in contemporary theory, with scholars from a variety of disciplines such as geography, urban studies, sociology, philosophy, and so on contributing to critical discussions on space. In examining the implications of the spatial turn, it becomes clear that while space-oriented thinkers are gaining more attention, there is a risk of rehashing old analyses in new terms rather than recognizing the transformative potential of this shift. At face value, the spatial turn means that thinkers with a spatial orientation are receiving increasing attention in larger theorizing on society, culture, politics, and economy. Similarly, figures from traditional spatial disciplines, such as geography, urban sociology, urban planning, urban studies, etc., are attaining transdisciplinary status and a wider epistemological influence. However, the far-reaching implications of the spatial turn can only be established when traced as a dialogue between traditional spatial disciplines and the rest of the humanities and social sciences, which results in a transforming and perhaps radicalizing of both. This means invigorating the empiricism of geography and urban studies with a critical apparatus. Scholars like Soja have built on Lefebvre's ideas, particularly in his *Postmodern Geographies: The Reassertion of Space in Critical Social Theory* (1989), where he traces the evolution of geography from descriptive empiricism to a more critical study of social space. Soja argues that space can be a tool for power, discipline, and ideological control, making it crucial to examine the politics embedded within seemingly neutral spaces. For literary and cultural scholars, the spatial turn offers a way to ground their analyses in the materiality of actual locations, facilitating a deeper understanding of how literary spaces relate to real-world contexts. Apart from the multidisciplinary approach, theories on space have also become concerned with multiple scales—the larger scales of cities and city-regions; the smaller scales of neighbourhoods and communities; and the smallest scales of the body and affect.

In this interdisciplinary framework, cities have emerged as central subjects of study in the context of globalization, with urban spaces increasingly serving as strategic hubs for global flows. Rather than being defined by the nation-state, cities are now viewed as the primary units of reterritorialization in a globalized world. Traditionally, geographers and urban planners have concentrated on issues like the size, density, aesthetics, and history of cities, as well as the interplay between the built environment and the social forces that shape it. A quick survey may lead to works such as V. Gordon Childe's "urban revolution," H.D.F. Kitto's exploration of the Greek polis, and Ernest Burgess's concentric zone model, which debate types of city structure. Lewis Mumford viewed cities as social institutions, while Kevin

Lynch's cognitive mapping emphasized mental maps in urban design. Jane Jacobs celebrated lively, mixed-use neighbourhoods, advocating for citizen participation in ensuring safety and critiquing modernist architecture, especially Le Corbusier's ideas. Constantin Doxiadis's "ekistics" proposed a Utopian city, "Ecumenopolis," which countered the decentralization promoted by Ebenezer Howard's "garden city" concept (LeGates and Stout, 1996). The rich, foundational approaches of these scholars have in many ways influenced much of the discursive theorizing on critical spatial studies. Their persistent enquiries into mitigating urban crises by making cities better places for their inhabitants to live in have attained wider and more political scope in the present scholarship on cities, as the problems of cities become symptomatic of the problems of larger society and political economy. One of the key areas where continuity might be forged is the question of establishing "rights to the city" by negotiating the dystopic urban space of massive alienation prompted by the spectrality of city-life and regulated by heightened state-sponsored surveillance. As Harvey says, "the right to the city" (2003) is not merely a right of access to what already exists, but a right to change it" (2003: 939). Mike Davis, in *City of Quartz: Excavating the Future in Los Angeles* (1990), envisions a bleak future for cities (specifically Los Angeles) with public spaces being increasingly encroached by private gated communities and systems of surveillance being operative as robust signs in regulating the movement of the undesirable "Other." It is no wonder that Foucault's concept of the "panopticon" and "heterotopia" are some of the major influences in research concerned with surveillance and the city.

In view of the interdisciplinary spatial turn and the rise in importance of cities, it is also important to ask what separates the moment of the contemporary global urban from earlier moments. Contemporary theorists of the city, especially those working within the ambit of globalization and the city, consider cities as the restructured space of transnational global capital, but their approaches vary to a great extent. Sassen (1991), in her path-breaking book, proposed the idea of global cities in the early 1990s. In the event of the simultaneous rise of sub-national units such as cities and regions, alongside supra-national structures like global digital markets and free trade blocs, Sassen considered the rise of global cities as strategic spatial units, which act as sites of centralized control in the global agglomeration economy, dependent on dispersed "service firms" that supplant the earlier hegemony of the nation-state. David Harvey's (1989) concept of "time-space compression," the product of the flexible accumulation of the postfordist economy giving rise to entrepreneurial cities to provide a "spatial fix" to peripatetic capital; Soja's six discourses on the postmetropolis; Manuel Castells's concept of "the space of flows" as a product of the informational economy that is disrupted by "the space of places" of the fixed labour shaping the matrix of the new age city; Doreen Massey's work on gendered aspects of the spaces of globalization; Mike Davis's (2007) apocalyptic analyses of the dismal urban involution climaxing in slum cities in the developing world; Neil Brenner's (2004) more nuanced understanding of the spatial restructuring of the transnational economic order by focusing on the re-scaling aspects of both the nation-state and the city in globalization; and Ash Amin and Nigel Thrift's considering of cities in globalization primarily as a fluid state of the affect of human and non-human actors are some of the several influential analyses of the space of the city in globalization.

Postcolonial studies have also not been completely immune to the spatial turn. As far as geographers are concerned, worth mentioning are Derek Gregory's tracing of Said's concept of "imaginative geographies"[5] in the material contexts of colonial Egypt in *Geographical Imaginations* (1994) and in *The Colonial Present* (2004), his exploring of the terrains of Afghanistan, Palestine, and Iraq as bearing the marks of the "colonial present" in the post 9/11 world. In *The Edge of the Empire: Postcolonialism and the City* (1996), Jane M. Jacobs's exploration of London and the Australian cities of Perth and Brisbane as an attempt to "move beyond the spatial rhetoric of colonial and postcolonial theory and return it to 'real geographies'" (Jacobs, 1996: x), or Alison Blunt and Cheryl McEwan's similar attempt in *Postcolonial Geographies* (2002) to counter the criticism that "postcolonialism is too theoretical and not rooted enough in material contexts" (Blunt and McEwan, 2002: 6) are also some of the more interesting works that have incisively engaged with the impact of the imperial agency in restructuring the landscape of the metropolis and the periphery alike. Their more nuanced attention to the materiality of spaces and built environment of cities have happily intervened in postcolonial literary studies and have prompted such texts as Sara Upstone's *Spatial Politics in the Postcolonial Novel* (2009) and her co-edited *Postcolonial Spaces: The Politics of Place in Contemporary Culture* (2011), with Andrew Teverson, which follow an interdisciplinary methodology rather than using spatial language innocently, metaphorically, or ornamentally. However, postcolonial scholars also critique the global city theory by challenging the Eurocentric focus on cities in the Global North, like New York, London, and Tokyo, which perpetuate a hierarchical view and marginalize cities in the Global South. Neil Brenner and Roger Keil's 2014 article critiques traditional global city theory by moving beyond simplistic hierarchical models. Instead of viewing global cities as a linear hierarchy based solely on economic factors, they propose understanding cities as nodes in complex, interlocking networks that encompass economic, political, cultural, and infrastructural dimensions. They emphasize that cities are not just economic centres but also key players in global cultural exchange, with some cities, known for their media and communication capabilities, influencing global perceptions and information flows.

Jennifer Robinson challenges the idea that global cities are defined solely by their economic power. In her influential book *Ordinary Cities: Between Modernity and Development* (2013), Robinson advocates for a more inclusive understanding of urban globalization, emphasizing the importance of cities in the Global South, which are often overlooked in traditional global city discussions. She proposes "comparative urbanism" to study cities across diverse contexts and critiques the Eurocentric focus of global city theory. In *Ordinary Cities* (2013), she promotes the concept of "ordinary cities," arguing that all cities, regardless of geopolitical positioning, should be understood as dynamic, with their own unique roles in social and economic life. Robinson critiques the developmentalism inherent in global city theory, which often implies that cities in the Global South should aspire to global status by adopting Western urban values.

Ananya Roy's work highlights the importance of historical context and social exclusion, particularly how low-income populations and informal economies are often neglected in global city discourses. Roy calls for a broader understanding of urban dynamics that includes informal and peripheral practices. Rashmi Varma's research offers critical insights into how colonial histories shape contemporary urban environments. In *The Postcolonial City and Its Subjects* (2011), she emphasizes the distinction between "global" and "postcolonial" categories, focusing on the resistant politics of marginalized subjects in postcolonial cities like London, Nairobi, and Bombay. Varma argues that these cities should be understood not only in terms of their global significance but also as spaces shaped by colonial legacies and resistant politics, especially feminist struggles. Claire Chambers and Graham Huggan (2015) also explore postcolonial cities, recognizing them as both modern and historical. They argue that these cities, while shaped by colonial pasts, offer dynamic models for the future. Postcolonial cities, they contend, are complex sites of contradiction, where modernity intersects with histories of marginality and resistance.

These critiques argue that global city theory imposes Western standards on non-Western cities, reflecting neocolonial power dynamics. Postcolonial critiques of global city theory reassess how cities are categorized in the context of globalization. The focus on a few cities in the Global North, such as New York, London, and Tokyo, perpetuates a hierarchical view that marginalizes cities in the Global South. Postcolonial scholars argue that this framework reflects a neocolonial power dynamic, where Western standards are imposed on other cities, disregarding their unique historical, social, and economic contexts. These critiques highlight how cities in the Global South develop innovative solutions that reflect local realities, challenging the homogenizing tendencies of global city theory. Postcolonial perspectives advocate for a more inclusive approach that values the diverse experiences of cities worldwide and recognizes their contributions to global urbanism.

This brief overview of some of the recent developments in research on space and the city is intended to demonstrate the eclecticism of studies on space in our times. Postcolonial studies have also engaged with the spatial turn and have argued for a more nuanced, postcolonial approach to urban studies, one that recognizes the complexity of cities in the Global South and challenges the binary between the Global North and South. This approach emphasizes the need to historicize globalization and understand the role of cities as centres of global flows both in the past and present. The rise of global cities, as theorized by Saskia Sassen and others, signals a new era where cities are central to the organization of global capital. However, as David Harvey, Manuel Castells, and others have shown, this new urban era is marked by contradictions and tensions. The "time-space compression" of global capitalism, the rise of entrepreneurial cities, and the shifting power dynamics between cities and nation-states all contribute to a complex landscape of urban transformation in the twenty-first century. The spatial turn has thus provided a critical framework for understanding the changing nature of cities, their role in globalization, and the ways in which they shape and are shaped by broader geopolitical, economic, and cultural forces.

Cities in Salman Rushdie's Novels

The passage from *The Moor's Last Sigh* contrasts Aurora Zogoiby with Nargis Dutt, highlighting Rushdie's relationship with cities and his portrayal of contrasting ideals:

> My mother was no Nargis Dutt—she was the in-your-face type, not serene. Catch her hauling a shovel over her shoulder! I am pleased to say that I have never seen a spade. Aurora was a city girl, perhaps the city girl, as much the incarnation of the smarty boots metropolis as Mother India was village earth made flesh.
>
> *(1995: 139)*

Nargis Dutt, an iconic actress in Indian cinema, portrayed the role of *Mother India* (1957), a strong and self-sacrificing village woman, embodying a model of nation-building focused on rural values. In contrast, Aurora Zogoiby, like Rushdie, represents the urbane, cosmopolitan individual. Rushdie uses this contrast to address the dichotomy between rural and urban India, where the village aligns with the Gandhian ideal of *Ram Rajya*—an idyllic, mythic state—and cities are tied to Nehruvian ideals of secularism, modernity, and progress. This contrast symbolizes the competing visions shaping India's postcolonial identity. However, modern scholarship has moved beyond the traditional debate about whether cities are out of place in a predominantly rural nation. With the post-liberalized India of the late twentieth and twenty-first centuries, both villages and cities play crucial roles, and writers like Rushdie, who primarily focus on cities, are now seen as contributing to the broader understanding of the urban experience in a globalized world. Scholars such as Rashmi Varma (2004) have analyzed how globalization and provincialization shape cities like Bombay in Rushdie's works, offering new perspectives on urban life.

In John Clement Ball's *Imagining London* (2004), London's role as a transnational metropolis is explored through the works of postcolonial writers, including Rushdie. Ball examines how these writers often reimagine London, both engaging with and resisting its imperial legacy. Writers like Rushdie find London familiar yet alien, crafting alternative narratives that reflect the experiences of the formerly colonized. Similarly, John McLeod (2004) discusses how postcolonial writers engage with "Postcolonial London," viewing it not just as a physical space shaped by colonial history but as a site of creative and oppositional thought. This approach recognizes London as a space that is continually reshaped by immigrants from former colonies, transforming it into a hybrid, contested terrain. Vassilena Parashkevova (2012) extends this analysis, examining how cities in Rushdie's novels reflect the global urban condition. She uses metaphors like "catoptrics" and "tectonic" to describe the mirror-like, dynamic qualities of cities in Rushdie's works. These cities are shaped by the travels of postcolonial migrants, and their representations in Rushdie's novels reflect both contemporary realities and historical tensions. Nicole Weickgenannt Thiara (2011) contrasts Rushdie's representation of Bombay with that of *The Enchantress of Florence*, highlighting the difference between an orchestrated, controlled hybridity and the chaotic, unruly hybridity of Bombay. This difference reveals how Rushdie's portrayal of cities reflects both the cultural diversity of India and the broader Global South, resisting the idealized notion of unity promoted by Nehru's nationalistic project. Stuti Khanna (2011) also explores how Rushdie's distinctive narrative style—characterized by a "chutnified" language—captures the vibrant, chaotic essence of Bombay. Khanna argues that this style is a direct response to the complexities of writing about a city like Bombay, where fluidity, disorder, and cultural fusion are fundamental to its identity. Khanna connects this linguistic and stylistic innovation to Rushdie's portrayal of artists like Saleem Sinai, Aurora Zogoiby, and Umeed Merchant, who are shaped by their socio-economic contexts and the urban environment in which they live. In a more recent work (2023), she says Salman Rushdie's work is deeply tied to urban landscapes, shaping his narratives through themes of infrastructure, crime, and corruption. Bombay/Mumbai remains central from *Midnight's Children* to *The Ground Beneath Her Feet*, while *The Satanic Verses* explores 1980s London. His later works, including *Fury*, *Two Years Eight Months and Twenty-Eight Nights*, and *The Golden House*, shift focus to New York. She examines how cityscapes influence Rushdie's storytelling, arguing that his formal techniques and linguistic innovations are best understood through the metropolis, where his key themes naturally emerge. Rufus Cook (1994) addresses the question of place in Rushdie's novels, specifically examining Karachi's portrayal. Cook's analysis considers whether Rushdie's works open up possibilities for engaging with geopolitics or create self-contained, intertextual worlds that distance themselves from real-world political concerns. This book seeks to explore cities in Rushdie's fiction as sites of alternative globalization by considering their roles within the larger dynamics of the global postcolonial urban experience. It adopts an interdisciplinary approach, blending literary analysis with social sciences to understand how Rushdie's cities contest contemporary global narratives. Rushdie's early works have often been analyzed through the lens of postcolonial nation-building, focusing on the successes and failures of India and Pakistan. This book shifts the focus to the cities in Rushdie's novels, exploring them through an alternative spatial perspective. The methodology used here is interdisciplinary, aiming to create a dialogic space between literary and social sciences while emphasizing the importance of cities in understanding globalization. The book challenges dominant discourses around globalization, particularly those privileging the Global North, by focusing on cities in the Global South, specifically through Rushdie's depictions of Bombay, Karachi, and other locales.

The book's first chapter provides an overview of existing scholarship on Rushdie and cities in the context of globalization. The chapter outlines key theoretical frameworks in critical spatial studies—drawing on Lefebvre, de Certeau, Soja, and Massey—to build an interdisciplinary approach that foregrounds space, place, and mobility in Rushdie's work, while also critiquing the limitations of applying global theories to postcolonial urban contexts. Chapter 2 contrasts Saskia Sassen's idea of the "global city" with Rushdie's portrayal of urban centres shaped by myth, memory, and Global South histories, using Soja's concept of *synekism* to examine tensions between creative, nomadic energies and institutional forces. Chapter 3 focuses on Bombay as a recurring setting in Rushdie's novels, interpreting it as a lived, affective space shaped by land reclamation and layered histories, offering a counterpoint to placeless globality and nostalgic essentialism. Chapter 4 analyzes representations of home in an era of displacement and globalization, arguing that Rushdie's literary homes act as *lieux de mémoire*—embodied, mnemonic spaces that resist alienation and commodification while remaining open to plural affiliations. Chapter 5 explores walking in Rushdie's narratives as a posthuman, resistant practice that entangles bodies, spaces, and histories, challenging dominant urban imaginaries through the fragmented, mobile perspectives of postcolonial subjects. Together, these chapters trace how Rushdie's fiction reimagines cities, homes, and bodies as dynamic, contested sites of memory, resistance, and global belonging. Through these contributions, the book provides a fresh understanding of Rushdie's work and its engagement with global cities.

2

REROUTING RUSHDIE'S NOVELS THROUGH LITERATURE ON GLOBAL SPACE AND CITIES

Introduction

> But the fact is that I am a boy who spent his life in gigantic rotting cities. They define me. I know very well that London and Bombay have much more in common with each other than either have with the hinterlands behind them. If I came from Bombay to London, I would recognize the city. A Londoner who goes to Bombay would recognize the city. If you are a city creature, you understand cities. You understand their artificiality and their transience, their internal contradictoriness. It's out of that that I've tried to build my writing, out of that experience of space and time that we have in the modern city.
>
> ("Keeping up with Salman Rushdie: James Fenton")

This chapter is divided into two distinct sections, each addressing critical aspects of the subject matter. The first section focuses on an in-depth exploration of the existing literature surrounding Salman Rushdie's novels, with particular attention to how cities are portrayed within them. Despite Rushdie's extensive exploration of themes such as migration, identity, and cultural hybridity, there has been a noticeable gap in scholarly research regarding the cities depicted in his works. Specifically, there is a lack of critical engagement with the role of these cities in the context of globalization. This gap serves as the entry point for initiating a broader discussion on how the urban landscapes in Rushdie's novels can be understood within the framework of global interconnectivity and urban transformation. The second section shifts focus to the theories surrounding space and the city, particularly in the context of globalization. This part delves into how cities are conceptualized in contemporary urban theory, particularly as globalization reshapes urban landscapes, identities, and social dynamics. It examines

DOI: 10.4324/9781003106180-2

the evolving theories that view cities not as isolated entities but as interconnected nodes in a global network of economic, cultural, and political flows. By understanding these theories, the chapter aims to provide a theoretical foundation for analyzing the cities in Rushdie's novels. This theoretical perspective also contributes to understanding how globalization impacts not only physical spaces but also the identity and experiences of individuals within these spaces. The theories discussed will offer a critical lens through which to explore the urban dimensions of Rushdie's works, bridging the gap between literature and urban theory in the context of global change.

A Review of the Critical Reception of Salman Rushdie's Works

Since the publication of *Midnight's Children* (1981), Salman Rushdie's novels have garnered extensive critical attention. However, a focused exploration of the cities depicted in his works—a central theme throughout his fiction—remains underexamined in contemporary scholarship. While a comprehensive analysis of the evolving body of Rushdie criticism spanning over three decades would be redundant for the scope of this book, it is vital to outline some key trends: Rushdie as a postcolonial writer, particularly with regard to themes of migrancy and hybridity; Rushdie as a postmodern writer; the reception of *The Satanic Verses* (1988) in the context of "The Rushdie Affair"; and the more recent assessment of Rushdie's stance on globalization and terrorism.

The evaluation of Rushdie as a postcolonial writer, although approached from various angles, primarily focuses on the "political" aspects of his work rather than the semiotic ones. Postcolonial scholars have particularly concentrated on Rushdie's depiction of postcolonial India and Pakistan from the perspective of the diasporic writer. Rushdie's ambivalence towards the postcolonial nation-state is perhaps most clearly reflected in the tension between form and content in *Midnight's Children*, a dynamic Rushdie himself references in *Imaginary Homelands* (1992: 16). The novel presents a pessimistic thematic portrayal of India, which is countered by the text's vibrant, "teeming" narrative, reflecting Rushdie's mixed feelings about the nation's birth and future. While he celebrates secular India built on Nehru's ideals, he also critiques the failure of this secular vision, highlighting the rise of fascist elements, such as Indira Gandhi's declaration of Emergency (in *Midnight's Children*) and sectarian politics, as seen in the Mumbai-based Shiv Sena in *The Moor's Last Sigh* (1995) and *The Ground Beneath Her Feet* (1999). However, as demonstrated in *Shame* (1983), Rushdie portrays Pakistan as being doomed by the dominance of religious extremism and authoritarianism since its inception. Timothy Brennan notes that, as a "Third-world Cosmopolitan" writer, Rushdie exposes the fragility of the postcolonial nation-state but does so in a way that caters to the demands of the First

World literary market (1989). Gyan Prakash takes a similar stance, focusing on Rushdie's interrogation of colonial historiography and the nation-state. Unlike Brennan, Prakash views Rushdie's approach as empowering, as Rushdie's "mythographies" allow him to "expose the mythic quality of the colonial and postcolonial fables of modernity" (1990: 405). In contrast, Neil ten Kortenaar argues that by "literarizing" the allegories of nation-states, Rushdie emphasizes their fictional nature, while paradoxically inviting a provisional belief in the very nation he deconstructs (1999: 29). Kortenaar's other work, *Self, Nation, Text in Salman Rushdie's Midnight's Children* (2004), further explores the complex relationship between national and cosmopolitan perspectives in Rushdie's novels. By revisiting themes such as hybridity, cosmopolitanism, and nationalism—especially in the context of India—Kortenaar asserts that these impulses are not binary opposites in Rushdie's works. Instead, they interact and reshape one another, as illustrated by the character of Saleem Sinai, to construct the notions of self, nation, and world throughout Rushdie's oeuvre.

Rushdie spent his childhood in Bombay, his adolescence and much of his adult life in London, with occasional visits to Pakistan, where his immediate family had relocated from India. He has been residing in New York since the late 1990s. His novels reflect the hybridization of various cultures that he has encountered throughout his life, embodying what he himself describes as a "melange, hodgepodge, a bit of this and a bit of that" (Rushdie, 1991: 394). Rushdie notes that writers who have "emigrated" often "feel that we straddle two cultures; at other times, that we fall between two stools" (1992: 15). However, this liminal position offers them a "stereoscopic vision," providing a "double perspective" from which to write, since they are simultaneously insiders and outsiders within society (1992: 19). As such, one of the most influential ways to understand Rushdie's conceptualization of the nation-state is through the discourse of hybridity and liminality, concepts introduced by Homi Bhabha in *The Location of Culture* (1994). Bhabha himself elaborates, stating that "Salman Rushdie writes the fabulist historiography of post-Independence India and Pakistan in *Midnight's Children* and *Shame*, only to remind us in *The Satanic Verses* that the truest eye may now belong to the migrant's double vision" (1994: 5).

Rushdie scholarship examining his creative use of the English language and the intertextuality in his works also engages with themes of postcoloniality, hybridity, and migration. His "chutnification" of English—incorporating occasional Hindi/Urdu words, creating "Hinglish" terms, and deliberately altering syntax—is viewed by some critics as an authentic representation of the postcolonial Indian subcontinent's reality (Bharucha, 1994: 159–172; Needham, 1988: 609–624; Bardolph, 1994: 209–220). However, critics such as Harish Trivedi argue that Rushdie's innovative use of language is merely a clever device to present an exoticized Indian flavour to a metropolitan audience (1999: 69–94). Taking a broader, extra-literary approach, Graham Huggan (2001) examines Rushdie's remarkable success with the Booker Prize (which he won for *Midnight's Children* in 1981, and later for *Booker of the Bookers* in 1993 and Best of the Bookers in 2008) in the context of the Booker Prize's tendency to exoticize postcolonial cultures for the First World literary market. Echoing Huggan, Anna Christina Mendes (2013), in her recent work, positions Rushdie within the cultural marketplace of the "brown cultural industry," focusing on the dynamics of the global production and consumption of his novels. Mendes observes that the "brand" Rushdie has been shaped by the global cultural industry's reification of South Asian culture.

The intertextuality in Rushdie's works further reinforces the hybrid nature of his artistry. Numerous critics have explored the influence of canonical Western writers such as Laurence Sterne (Wilson, 1994: 55–68; Alter, 1999: 112–116), Rudyard Kipling (Cronin, 1999: 134–148), Gunter Grass (Merivale, 1999: 116–133), and James Joyce (Booker, 1990: 977–997), as well as Western literary genres such as Satire (in the vein of Rabelais, Jonathan Swift, and Sterne, tracing back to Menippean satire) and the Gothic (Teverson, 2003), or its postcolonial adaptations, on Rushdie's writing. However, the counterclaim that Rushdie has also been influenced by Indian and Eastern elements is equally compelling. Critics have identified the influence of ancient Indian texts such as the Mahabharata (Brennan, 1989; Syed, 1999: 149–164), Kathasaritsagar, and Panchatantra (Durix, 1993: 121; Cundy, 1994: 339; Mukherjee, 1998: 167), as well as works of Islamic lineage such as the *Arabian Nights* (Batty, 1999: 95–113) and Sufi traditions like Farid-ud-din Attar's *The Conference of Birds* (Brennan, 1989; Teverson, 2001: 444–466; Aji, 1995: 103–129). Additionally, the dastan narrative tradition (Jussawalla, 1996: 50–73) has been noted as an influence on Rushdie. While not specifically literary, critics such as Vijay Mishra (2007: 11–28; 2012: 112–128) have also commented extensively on the influence of *Bombay Talkies* on Rushdie's novels. Indeed, it is challenging to clearly demarcate the Eastern and Western influences in Rushdie's writing, as they are intricately interwoven, much like the various threads of the Sea of Stories in *Haroun and the Sea of Stories* (1990). Mishra (2020) in a recent work shows how Rushdie combines a new form of English with Indian, Arabic, and Persian traditions, creating a distinctive orientalism that defines his humanism within world literature. Mishra connects Rushdie to both radical non-Western humanism and English-European sensibilities, arguing that understanding his work requires uncovering the "genesis of secrecy" through a close reading of not only his texts but also his archive. It is the first book to situate a critical work through an extensive exploration of the Salman Rushdie archive at Emory University.

To highlight Rushdie's hybridity, one can refer to the debate surrounding his adherence to the genre of magic realism, which was popularized by the Latin American writer Gabriel García Márquez. Scholars such as Sadik J. Al-Azm (1994: 255–292) and Patricia Merivale (1999: 116–133) have specifically pointed to García Márquez's influence on Rushdie, noting his seamless blending of the natural and supernatural in his novels, which is often attributed to the genre of magic realism. However, Rushdie himself offers an alternative source for his use of the fantastical: the fabulous tales his father, Anis Rushdie, told him as bedtime stories during his childhood (Rushdie, 2012: 19). Rushdie's novels merge his deep connection to Indian Muslim heritage with a broader cosmopolitan perspective. This produces an innovative narrative style that blends poetic language with storytelling in a non-linear, mosaic-like structure. This fragmented style mirrors both the modern borderless world and India's complex ethnic and religious diversity, which remains unfused—unlike the unified national identities formed in nineteenth-century Europe. Amid India's competing societal demands and the chaos of globalization, Rushdie's characters navigate uncertain and unpredictable journeys. Thus, Rushdie occupies a unique in-between space—straddling both Eastern and Western worlds—and this position is firmly reflected in the literary traditions he is believed to follow.

While Rushdie is frequently considered a postcolonial writer by scholars in the field, he has also been categorized as postmodern. Scholars like David Birch have referred to *Midnight's Children* as "postmodernist chutney," describing it as a playful mixture of signs that eschews the burden of meaning creation (1991: 1–7). In contrast, D.M. Fletcher argues that Rushdie engages in "postmodern writing of a humorous and biting variety," suggesting that Rushdie's novels have a satiric intent (1994: 8). A critical and influential perspective comes from Linda Hutcheon, whose groundbreaking study categorizes Rushdie's novels as "historiographic metafiction." Hutcheon acknowledges that while Rushdie's works are "self-referential" and align with postmodernist characteristics, they paradoxically retain an operative historicity (1988). Unlike Fredric Jameson, who views the intertextuality and quoting of genres in postmodern works as indicative of fragmented subjectivity, Hutcheon's concept of "parody" allows for the past to be both inscribed and subverted. In her words, "the structure of the parody enables that past to be admitted as inscribed, but also subverted at the same time" (Hutcheon, 1988: 100). She further explains that "parody becomes a way of ironically revisiting the past—of both art and history—in a novel like *Midnight's Children* with its double parodic intertext: Grass's *The Tin Drum* and Sterne's *Tristram Shandy*" (Hutcheon, 1988: 99). Thus, while Hutcheon clearly situates Rushdie within the postmodern tradition, her emphasis on the historicity of his novels imbues them with a political impulse, aligning her critique with postcolonial scholars such as Rukmini Bhaya Nair (1999: 49–68) and Uma Parameswaran (1982: 52–60, 1983: 34–45), who have explored Rushdie's subversive use of history. More recently, Søren Frank (2011) examines Salman Rushdie's novels through the philosophical framework of Gilles Deleuze, particularly focusing on themes of migration, identity, and multiplicity. By applying Deleuzian concepts such as deterritorialization, becoming, and rhizomatic structures, Frank interprets Rushdie's works as fluid, constantly shifting narratives that resist fixed identities or singular interpretations. Rushdie's storytelling aligns with Deleuze's notion of the rhizome—a non-hierarchical, interconnected system—where characters, histories, and myths intertwine in non-linear and fragmented ways. Frank also highlights how Rushdie's novels enact deterritorialization, where individuals and societies are uprooted from stable origins and forced into new, dynamic states of existence. In this context, Rushdie's works reject rigid national, religious, and historical boundaries, embracing a postmodern, globalized vision. His characters experience continuous transformation, mirroring Deleuze's idea of "becoming"—an ongoing, unpredictable process of identity formation. Frank in an earlier work considers Rushdie's novels as "schizo-novels constantly migrating" (2008: 176). According to him, Rushdie's works reflect a globalized world defined by cultural dispersion—a concept Frank cleverly terms "dissemiNation."

Although not as dominant, another significant strand of Rushdie scholarship addresses his treatment of women in his novels. Catherine Cundy points out that "Rushdie's problematic depictions of women appear as a thread running through his work, seemingly trivial in isolation but disturbing with their cumulative weight," and notes that his female characters often appear trapped in the "innocent/whore binarism" (1993: 13). Keith M. Booker, however, offers a different perspective, arguing that Rushdie's fiction embraces contradiction, privileging the plural over the singular and the polyphonic over the monologic. According to Booker, one of the clearest ways Rushdie achieves this is through constructing dual oppositions—similar to the snakes and ladders game in *Midnight's Children*—and then deconstructing these oppositions by demonstrating that the apparent polar opposites are in fact interchangeable and mutually interdependent (1990: 978). This interpretation allows us to read an ironic intention in the apparent dualism in Rushdie's characterization of women. In this light, scholars like Justyna Deszcz have read *Shame* as a "postmodern feminist subversion of the master narrative of Euro-American androcentric culture" (2004: 27). Related to this discussion are the works of critics such as Nalini Natarajan (1999: 165–181), Alexandra W. Schultheis (2004: 105–151), and Amina

Yaqin (2007: 61–75), who have explored how Rushdie's portrayal of women and family is intricately tied to his conceptualization of the postcolonial nation-state.

The critical trends discussed above have largely focused on evaluating Rushdie's works through various literary lenses. However, following the fatwa issued by Iran's Ayatollah Khomeini on 14 February 1989, which decreed the assassination of Rushdie for his authorship of *The Satanic Verses*, a significant portion of Rushdie scholarship has been framed through what is referred to as "The Rushdie Affair." Since 1989, Rushdie has transcended the role of a mere writer, transforming into both a "cause" and, more recently, a global celebrity, particularly after the conclusion of the Ayatollah's persecution (which involved considerable violence). As Gayatri Spivak aptly notes, attempting a closed literary reading of *The Satanic Verses* is "to attempt the impossible…as if nothing has happened since late 1988" (1989: 219). In more recent scholarship, Ruvani Ranasinha (2007: 45–60) has renewed the discussion surrounding *The Satanic Verses*, emphasizing the differential interpretations of the novel within Muslim communities, especially among poor, non-reading Muslims in Bradford, by deconstructing the aesthetic category of fiction. The reception of *The Satanic Verses*, particularly after the fatwa, has often been framed as a conflict between Western secularism and Eastern fundamentalism. Balanced scholarly evaluations, such as those by Edward Said (1989: 17–18) and Srinivas Aravamudan (1989: 3–20), while condemning the actions of the Muslim protestors who targeted Rushdie, have also critiqued the often partial and vacuous nature of Western values like liberty, free speech, and secularism, especially in relation to the Islamic world. Anshuman Mondal (2014) has similarly interrogated the value of free speech, particularly as it became synonymous with Rushdie after *The Satanic Verses* controversy, questioning whether such values are universally applicable or context-dependent. In this vein, scholars like Sara Suleri (1994: 221–236) and Aamir Mufti (1991: 95–116) have situated Rushdie as a postcolonial writer who engages with Islam in a complex and problematic manner, rather than embodying the ideals of Western secularism in opposition to Islamic fundamentalism. Reza Afshari (1991: 107–114) similarly defends Rushdie against critics like Ali Mazrui (1989: 19–32), who labelled *The Satanic Verses* as "hate literature" comparable to Hitler's *Mein Kampf*. However, these critics largely overlook the indigenous poetics in Rushdie's work, which are closely tied to the novel's impact on Islamic politics. On the other hand, critics such as Daniel Pipes (1990: 77–84) and Saadi A. Simawe (1990: 185–198) have contextualized *The Satanic Verses* within the long tradition of heretical literature in Islam. Feroza Jussawalla (1996: 50–73) offers a nuanced reading, interpreting *The Satanic Verses* as Rushdie's "dastan-e-dilruba," or love letter to Islam, and positioning Rushdie as both a postcolonial and post-Mughal writer. Jussawalla suggests that Rushdie's work, while often read as blasphemous, is actually a reformist attempt to reclaim Islam's history "out of love for his religion and his forefathers" (1996: 63). She contends that *The Satanic Verses* (along with other novels like *Midnight's Children*, *Shame*, and *Haroun and the Sea of Stories*) is not just a novel but a *dastan*, drawing from the traditions of poets like Ghalib, Hali, and Mir (1996: 64–71).

The first phase of Rushdie criticism focused on the literary evaluation of his texts, while the second phase centred on the extraliterary issues surrounding the fatwa. A newer, third phase has emerged, seeking to situate Rushdie within the context of the contemporary globalized world. For instance, Mariam Pirbhai in her article "The Paradox of Globalization as an 'Untotalizable Totality' in Salman Rushdie's *The Ground Beneath Her Feet*" (2001) analyzes *The Ground Beneath Her Feet* in the context of globalization, illustrating what she calls the "paradox of globalization," where the process of globalization both opens up the world to heterogeneous cultures and identities while simultaneously imposing hegemonic economic and cultural practices that force national and cultural entities to resist. Similarly, Florian Stadtler's analysis (2009) of *Shalimar the Clown* explores how the novel's use of terms like "terrorism" and "terror" challenges traditional postcolonial discourse, shifting the focus to a transnational perspective. Ágnes Györke (2023) underscores how Rushdie's fiction engages with globalization, a key theme in his work since *The Moor's Last Sigh*. His novels, including *The Moor's Last Sigh*, *The Ground Beneath Her Feet*, and *Fury*, explore the global movement of people, goods, and culture. Analyzing both their aesthetics and broader cultural contexts, she argues that Rushdie's post-fatwa novels reflect a shift in his perspective on globalization. Treasa De Loughry (2023) examines how Salman Rushdie's fiction narrates the history of global capitalism. From *The Enchantress of Florence* and its depiction of early modern Mughal and Florentine world systems to *Midnight's Children*'s portrayal of India's independence and emerging neoliberalism, and *The Golden House*'s exploration of transnational elites, Rushdie's work reflects shifting views on the world system. She shows how Rushdie uses different narrative techniques to capture the rise of neoliberalism and the decline of US hegemony in the globalized world. Manjeet Kumar Kashyap (2004) posits that Salman Rushdie's *Fury* explores the challenges migrants face due to Americanization and globalization. While America represents a land of opportunity, migrants struggle with identity, ethnicity, and cultural imposition. The novel critiques globalization as a tool for capitalist and Western dominance, showing how migrants resist but ultimately undergo acculturation despite their efforts. In a recent study, Dhee Sankar (2024) reads a shift from the postcolonial to posthuman sensibilities in Rushdie's novels. Sankar analyzes two novels of Salman Rushdie, *The Moor's Last Sigh* and *Two Years Eight Months and Twenty-Eight Nights*, to show how the trope of "war of the worlds" reflects a postcolonial dilemma, symbolizing an impending clash of civilizations in the former novel, and a comic, fantastical framework, addressing environmental catastrophes in the latter. By examining these texts together, the article highlights Rushdie's evolving use of the "war of the worlds" trope, moving from postcolonial concerns to global, apocalyptic posthuman themes.

Despite extensive scholarship on Rushdie, there remains a need for a more rigorous analysis of his nuanced and ironic portrayal of globalization, offering deeper insights into both his works and contemporary realities. Rushdie's earlier novels, such as *Midnight's Children*, *Shame*, and *The Satanic Verses*, were written in the 1980s, when twenty-first-century globalization was only beginning to take shape. However, his later works, starting from the late 1990s, engage more directly with globalization as a lived reality. Examining the cities in Rushdie's fiction requires consideration of postcolonial literature's discourse on the nation-state, hybridity, cosmopolitanism, and liminality—concepts Edward Soja describes as "inherently spatial" (1989: 35).

This book departs from previous research in two key ways. First, it shifts the analytical focus from the nation-state to the city, reflecting the evolving spatial dynamics of globalization. By treating cities as alternative spaces of belonging and displacement, the book highlights themes of homelessness and deterritorialization in Rushdie's fiction. Second, it critiques the tendency of postcolonial literary analysis to privilege "theory-driven spaces" over real, historically and geographically situated locales. Instead, this study broadens the discussion of Rushdie's spatiality by integrating historical, cultural, and geographical contexts. The next section introduces key interdisciplinary spatial theories that will provide the foundational framework for this book. While thinkers on globalization and the city differ in their approaches, they all address the simultaneous processes of homogenization and fragmentation in the spaces of networked economies. They discuss the pervasive alienation within the cities' spectral built environments, the erosion of security associated with a sense of place in the face of widespread placelessness, and the rise of new, strategic approaches to place-making. These strategies involve a variety of scales, from the micro-level of the body to larger levels such as the community and city. In essence, these scholars explore the "new" space of globalization—its deterritorializations and reterritorializations, as well as its resulting spatial inequalities, injustices, and forms of resistance and adaptation. This book delves into the core theoretical ideas of some of the most influential thinkers shaping contemporary understandings of cities in the globalized world. Reflecting the spatial turn, the selection of theorists is diverse, drawing on philosophers, geographers, sociologists, literary critics, and cultural theorists.

The Production of Space and Everyday Life

Henri Lefebvre's seminal work, *The Production of Space* (1991, originally published 1974), has been fundamental in reshaping the ontological and epistemological approach to space, particularly in the context of globalization and urban theory. Lefebvre builds on the notion of production, borrowing from Hegel, Marx, and Engels, to challenge the view of space as an empty container or a mere relation between things. Instead, he argues that space is produced through social processes and is inherently social. Lefebvre posits that the focus of spatial studies should be on "social space" rather than "physical" or "mental" space. Lefebvre famously declares that "(social) space is a (social) product," at once hegemonic and the site of resistance (1991: 27). He observes that the "mental space" of philosophers and mathematicians is opposed to physical space "as defined by the practico-sensory activity and the perception of nature" (1991: 27). In other words, Lefebvre is referring to the opaque natural space, which has been the basis of the study of such disciplines as empirical geography. Theories emanating from the illusion of the mental space that he terms as "illusion of transparency" and the illusion of the physical space that he terms as "realistic illusion" are instrumental in concealing social space. The "illusion of transparency," enables a design to be imposed upon social space and valorizes a fetishized (according to Lefebvre "innocent") space, which is the result of interpretations of such designs. On the other hand, the "illusion of opacity" is the result of "illusion of natural simplicity," which has been discarded by sophisticated theories of language and philosophy because of its appeal to "naturalness and substantiality" (1991: 29). To understand social space more clearly, Lefebvre introduces a triad consisting of spatial practice (perceived), representations of space (conceived), and representational space (lived space):

1. Spatial practice: The spatial practice produces, although not by design, the space of society at the level of perception, action, and materiality.
2. Representations of space: These are the abstract and often institutionalized conceptions of space, often tied to systems of power and control.
3. Representational space: This is the lived experience of space, rooted in everyday practices and the rhythms of daily life, offering potential for resistance and transformation.

Lefebvre also explores the importance of everyday life in his volume *Critique of Everyday Life* (originally published in 1947 translated in 2008). He argues that while modernity renders everyday life homogeneous, repetitive, and fragmented, it also holds the potential for revealing the extraordinary within the ordinary. This everyday life becomes the yardstick of revolution. His concept of rhythmanalysis seeks to capture the rhythms of daily life, particularly in the context of the tension between cyclical natural time and linear technocratic time. Lefebvre's insights on cities are found in *The Urban Revolution* (2003, originally published in 1970) and *Writings on Cities* (1996, originally published in 1968). His exploration of urbanism is both diachronic, tracking the evolution from rural to industrial to urban, and synchronic, analyzing the contemporary urban condition on various scales—from global to private. These works also introduce his concept of the "right to the city," a progressive call for the continuous enfranchisement of urban dwellers through the politics of habitation.

Time-Space Compression and the City

David Harvey extends Lefebvre's work through a political economy lens, viewing the city as a product of capital circulation. Harvey's approach centres on the fragmented and instrumentalized space of the city, shaped by speculative capital investments and resulting in urban problems such as uneven development and gentrification. He also addresses the entrepreneurial drive of cities, where competition for investment turns the built environment into "symbolic capital." In *The Condition of Postmodernity* (1989), Harvey introduces the concept of time-space compression to describe how advancements in transportation and communication technologies have shortened time and space. This process, he argues, has disrupted both economic practices and social life, creating intense competition between cities and regions. The collapse of spatial barriers, through accelerated turnover of capital, has led to an increasingly uniform global cityscape. However, Harvey is critical of the idea of "place-bound identity" as a form of resistance, fearing it might lead to the romanticized preservation of outdated identities.

Postmodern Geography

Building on Henri Lefebvre's work, Edward Soja extends the study of space beyond David Harvey's tradition of political economy into the realm of critical cultural theory. In advancing the manifesto of "postmodern" geography, Soja's approach is more eclectic than Harvey's, actively engaging with poststructuralist and feminist scholarship. His seminal work, *Postmodern Geographies: The Reassertion of Space in Critical Social Theory* (1989), explores the intersection of history and geography in modernity, tracing this relationship from the *fin de siècle* to contemporary times. As the subtitle suggests, Soja's primary aim is to emphasize the significance of social space in critical thought, particularly in an era of simultaneity and extension, where "human geography not only 'matters' but provides the most revealing critical perspective" (1989: 23).

Soja challenges traditional historicism, which he argues creates a "critical silence" around geographical interpretation. In contrast, he proposes:

> an appropriate interpretive balance between space, time and social being or what may now more explicitly be termed the creation of human geographies, the making of history, and the constitution of society.
>
> *(1989: 23)*

To reinforce his argument on the centrality of social space in critical thought, Soja adapts and reworks some of Lefebvre's concepts. His notions of the "illusion of transparency" and the "illusion of opaqueness" (1989: 118–137) extend Lefebvre's "illusion of transparency" and "realistic illusion." Similarly, his trialectics of spatiality and the theorization of "third space" in *Thirdspace: Journeys to Los Angeles and Other Real-and-Imagined Places* (1996) build upon Lefebvre's spatial triad. In *Postmetropolis: Critical Studies of Cities and Regions* (2000), Soja's analysis of Los Angeles as a postmetropolis and his six discourses on postindustrial cities—flexcity, cosmopolis, expolis, metropolarities, carceral archipelago, and simcities—offer valuable insights into understanding the dynamics of contemporary global urbanism.

The Global City and Gendered Geographies

Saskia Sassen's concept of the "global city," outlined in *The Global City: New York, London, Tokyo* (1991), highlights the role of cities in the transnational economy. Sassen argues that the rise of global cities as strategic spatial units reflects the decentralization of economic activities, where cities act as central nodes in global networks. This emergence of global cities signals a shift in the centrality of urban spaces, suggesting that they now function as "transterritorial centres" of power in a hypermobile informational economy. Doreen Massey, in *A Global Sense of Place* (1994), addresses the intersection of time-space compression with issues of gender and mobility. She critiques the tendency to romanticize place-based identities, which can obscure the inequalities that shape access to mobility. Massey argues for a more dynamic understanding of place, one that integrates the global and the local and sees places as processes shaped by multiple flows. She emphasizes that power relations—including those of gender—shape how different individuals experience movement, spatial belonging, and displacement. This rethinking of space resists homogenizing narratives of globalization and opens up possibilities for more inclusive and situated spatial politics. Her later work,

For Space (2005), further develops this idea, emphasizing space as a site of "radical heterogeneities."

Geographies of Everyday

Michel de Certeau (1984) explores the everyday life within modernity, which has been reshaped and disciplined by larger structural forces, a concept that echoes the work of Henri Lefebvre. Like Lefebvre, de Certeau identifies the repetitive, monotonous aspects of the everyday, suggesting that its complexities and residual elements defy full categorization. These residuals, he argues, are the source of transformation within daily life. However, unlike Lefebvre, de Certeau refrains from a socio-political "reform" of the everyday based on rationality. Instead, he focuses on the (often unconscious) subversive tactics that emerge within everyday practices, framing them as a kind of aesthetic resistance. De Certeau's method is to uncover the poetics of daily life, which can inspire a form of resistance that is not imposed externally but originates within the routines and interactions of the everyday.

In his seminal essay "Walking in the City" (1984: 91--110), de Certeau explores how the act of walking in the city creates a "mobile" city—one shaped by personal memories, stories, and myths. This movement allows for a form of resistance to the abstract, imposed urban spaces from above. The essay begins with a view from the World Trade Center, symbolizing a detached, privileged perspective over the city. From this position, the city appears as a totalized, distant object—unreachable, removed from the lived reality of the streets. De Certeau contrasts this distanced view with the active, immersive experience of walking, which allows one to engage with the city's streets and people, to participate in the unfolding everyday life. His critique of the observer's elevated position, which he associates with a voyeuristic detachment, stresses the importance of immersing oneself in the urban flow, where distinctions between author and spectator blur. However, de Certeau is also aware that the city's private histories and the personal connections walkers form with their surroundings are increasingly at risk of being homogenized by the media's global reach, thus diminishing the individuality of those everyday associations.

Critique of Globalization and Global Theories of Space and the City

The city has emerged as a key spatial unit in postmodern globalization, taking on greater significance than nation-states in shaping political economy, culture, and a sense of belonging. For theorists like Lefebvre (2003), the evolution of society from rural to industrial to urban calls for a focus on the process of "urbanization," rather than merely the concept of the "urban." In the current global age, cities act as nodes in networks, simultaneously acting as places and "spatial fixes" for global capital (Harvey, 1989). These cities, while sites of alienation, also become arenas for new forms of resistance that emerge from the body's affective encounters with the urban environment.

While these global theories are important, much of the scholarship has focused on cities in the Global North, such as New York, London, Tokyo, and Los Angeles. In contrast, scholars have sought to examine the cities of the Global South by historicizing globalization and tracing the central role these cities played before European hegemony. Justin Jennings (2012) challenges the perception of ancient cities as purely pre-capitalist spaces, presenting evidence of global interactions in ancient centres like Uruk and the Mississippian city. Similarly, historians like Felipe Fernández-Armesto (2006) and scholars like Sheldon Pollock (2000) contest the Eurocentric narrative of exploration and cosmopolitanism, highlighting the global interconnections in the ancient world that predate European dominance. Scholars like Walter Mignolo (2000) critique the Eurocentric framework that often ties globalization to European colonialism, proposing that contemporary globalization must be understood as part of a broader history of hegemonic colonial-modernity. Immanuel Wallerstein's World-System approach is revised by Janet Abu-Lughod (1989), who demonstrates how, prior to European ascendency, the East was integral to the world system. This broader, historically grounded understanding of globalization challenges the narrow Eurocentric view. Another approach to contesting global North-centric theories is to focus on the cities of the South from within, analyzing how contemporary global cities in the South challenge or complicate the postcolonial frameworks that often overlook local struggles. Simon Gikandi (2001) critiques celebratory accounts of globalization that treat multiculturalism and hybridity as benign outcomes, ignoring the more sinister aspects of globalization that marginalize the poor. Similarly, Simon During (1998) distinguishes between reconciliatory and critical postcolonialism, urging that contemporary struggles should be rooted in location-based politics rather than abstract global processes. Arif Dirlik (2002) argues that the forces of globalization have rendered traditional postcolonial struggles obsolete, as global capital now operates through performative networks rather than through the older imperial binaries. This global capital operates within what Hardt and Negri (2000) describe as "Empire," a phase where traditional notions of the centre and periphery are dissolved, giving rise to the "Multitude," a collective resistance that emerges from within globalization itself. Focusing specifically on the urban condition in globalization, scholars like Gyan Prakash (2011) and Arjun Appadurai (2000, 2011) explore how cities like Bombay (Mumbai) engage with global capital, offering alternative modernities. Prakash resists the metropolitan reading of Bombay by focusing on the city's mythic, anecdotal, and ethnographic dimensions.

Appadurai analyzes Bombay's housing crisis, illustrating how speculative capital, informal economies, and ethnic violence intersect to create a complex urban landscape.

As the discussion of global cities and the dynamics of globalization unfolds, we must now turn to another crucial aspect of contemporary urbanization: land reclamation. The processes of land transformation, such as those seen in coastal cities and megacities, reshape both physical spaces and the socio-political landscapes of urban environments. This concept intersects with Salman Rushdie's vision of a global sense of place, which we will explore in the next chapter. Through Rushdie's works, we can delve into the implications of these transformations, both literal and metaphorical, in constructing new forms of belonging and identity in an increasingly globalized world.

3

ALTERNATIVE GEOHISTORIES OF GLOBAL CITIES IN SALMAN RUSHDIE'S NOVELS

Edward Soja's concept of *synekism*—the stimulus of urban development through the proximity and interaction of diverse peoples and institutions—proves especially fruitful in understanding the distinct trajectories of urban formation in Rushdie's work. This chapter draws on Soja's spatial thinking to examine how moments of urban agglomeration in Rushdie's novels foreground a dynamic contestation between two opposing forces: matriarchal, nomadic, and fluid energies, often associated with creative and transformative potential; and paternalistic, statist, and institutionalizing impulses, linked to control, surveillance, and power consolidation. These tensions not only animate the imaginative geographies within Rushdie's narratives but also resonate with the competing spatial logics at play in the making of contemporary postmodern global cities.

Introduction

> The city was a man's space, a geometry of power and control, but under its surfaces ran older, darker, more chaotic forces, irrational and feminine, that refused to be mapped or ruled.
>
> (*The Ground Beneath Her Feet* 1999)

Salman Rushdie's novels offer a revisionist perspective on the geohistories of global cities, challenging conventional narratives. Global city theories, particularly those proposed by Saskia Sassen (1991), highlight a select group of cities in the Global North as strategic nodes of economic and spatial control, superseding the traditional dominance of nation-states. These theories frame contemporary globalization as a product of post-Fordist flexible accumulation, often detached from historical continuities. Their focus on

DOI: 10.4324/9781003106180-3

the synchronicity of global cities tends to obscure the deep-rooted material and cultural connections shaping urban networks over time. In contrast, Rushdie's novels foreground cities of the Global South—ranging from pre-Islamic Jahilia and Mughal Sikri to postcolonial Bombay and Karachi—as dynamic, interconnected sites of exchange and transformation. The cities of the Global North are primarily viewed through the lens of migration, disrupting Western canonical notions of time and space and reconfiguring their significance within global histories. This chapter employs Edward Soja's concept of synekism—the generative force of urban agglomeration that drives the development of all spatial units—as a framework for exploring alternative interconnections and hierarchies of urban formations in Rushdie's novels. Soja's analysis of Çatalhöyük and Jericho, two of the earliest cities emerging in south-central Anatolia and the Jordan Valley around 9,000–10,000 years ago, presents them as products of matriarchal and nomadic inclusivity rather than the exclusionary, paternalistic structures of the state. Building on Soja's insights, this chapter examines how Rushdie's cities embody an ongoing interplay between these matriarchal and nomadic forces of inclusivity and the patriarchal tendencies of institutionalization and exclusion. This dynamic produces a vision of global cities that, while amorphous and postmodern, remain distinctly shaped by historical and cultural differences.

The City in Globalization and Postcolonial Theory

The concept of the "global city" has been central to discussions of late twentieth- and early twenty-first-century urban development. Its widespread influence stems from theories that examine the production of networked space, processes of reterritorialization and deterritorialization, and the emergence of new inequalities and hierarchies in global urban formations. While these approaches effectively analyze globalization and its impact on cities in the contemporary era, they exhibit significant limitations when addressing the cities of the Global South. Saskia Sassen's work primarily focuses on New York, London, and Tokyo as dominant nodes in the global agglomeration economy, while Edward Soja and Mike Davis concentrate on Los Angeles, particularly its metropolitan region. This northern-centric focus positions cities of the Global North as the standard against which the progress of cities in the Global South is measured. Moreover, the emphasis on synchronicity in global city theories overlooks the historical connections and global engagements of southern cities in pre-modern and early modern periods, independent of European influence.

An alternative approach to understanding global urban networks would involve historicizing globalization and tracing decentralized global flows that bypass Europe. Scholars such as Janet Abu-Lughod (1989), Sheldon

Pollock (2000), and Walter Mignolo (2000), along with historians and cultural theorists studying Indian Oceanic connections, have played a crucial role in reconstructing these alternative histories of interconnectivity in the Global South. Another approach, more aligned with the objectives of this book, involves examining how postcolonial literary and cultural studies engage with the global cities paradigm. Postcolonial studies have long emphasized the "difference" and "otherness" of non-Western cultures in contrast to metropolitan centres, challenging dominant narratives through acts of contestation. Edward Said's *Orientalism* (1978) and *Culture and Imperialism* (1993) highlight the importance of spatial and territorial questions in understanding the power dynamics between the active West and the passive Orient. Likewise, Homi Bhabha's concept of the interstitial "third space" (1994), influenced by theorists such as Henri Lefebvre and Michel Foucault, resonates with Edward Soja's plural and fluid Third Space (1996) and Mary Louise Pratt's "contact zone" (1992). However, these spatial metaphors in postcolonial studies have been critiqued for their textual abstraction and detachment from material realities. Addressing this concern, Andrew Teverson and Sara Upstone (2011) seek to validate these metaphorical spaces through an engagement with Soja's more tangible Third Space, grounding postcolonial scholarship in the lived experiences of real-world urban spaces. Such efforts signal a shift in postcolonial literary and cultural studies, fostering greater methodological awareness and bridging the gap between theoretical discourse and place-based politics.

Saskia Sassen's model of global cities, with its rigorous engagement with spatial theories, has found traction in postcolonial studies, though often in a critical light. Ashley Dawson and Brent Hayes Edwards (2004) argue that Sassen's emphasis on New York, London, and Tokyo centralizes specific global metropolises in a way that tacitly aligns the progress of cities in the Global South with state-backed capitalist development models. Furthermore, global city theories tend to marginalize the cultural production of urban spaces by analyzing them primarily through superstructural frameworks, thereby limiting the scope for exploring the unique characteristics of cities in the Global South. Consequently, studies of former colonial cities in the twenty-first century often revolve around a recurring debate: should they be understood as postcolonial cities that continue to reenact the "colonial present" (Gregory, 2004) or as global cities reshaped by transnational capital? Rashmi Varma (2012), a feminist literary critic, insists on maintaining a clear distinction between the categories of "global" and "postcolonial" in her analysis of contemporary London, Nairobi, and Bombay. She argues that the "postcolonial" framework is crucial as it highlights the resistant politics of marginalized feminist subjects, who are often erased in dominant narratives of cities shaped by Western modernities. In contrast, urban studies scholars such as Ananya Roy and Aihwa Ong (2009) focus on Asian cities, examining their unique informal economies and interlinkages without explicitly categorizing their work as either a "hegemonic" globalization approach or a "resistant" postcolonial approach.

Anthropologist Arjun Appadurai (1996) offers another perspective, concentrating on the "disjunctures" and "differences" of global modernity as they manifest in the Global South. He navigates the debate without relying on the retrospective gaze often critiqued in postcolonial studies. His later works (2000, 2011) specifically examine the cultural economy of cities like Bombay, arguing that third-world cities are not merely subjected to the hegemonic forces of globalization but also appropriate and reshape these forces to produce alternative modernities. These spectral modernities accommodate both grassroots cosmopolitanisms and the exclusionary, often disruptive politics of neo-conservative parties such as the Shiv Sena. Building on Appadurai's framework, Caroline Herbert (2012) examines the spectral presence of marginalized figures in Bombay's transition to a global metropolis through literary analyses of Rushdie's *The Moor's Last Sigh* (1995) and Vikram Chandra's *Sacred Games* (2006). According to Herbert, these phantoms of the city keep alive the traces of absent-yet-present peripheralized citizen-subjects, sustaining a sense of postcolonial haunting within the emerging global metropolis. Similarly, Gillian Gane (2002) employs Sassen's global city framework to analyze how Rushdie articulates the tensions between postcolonial migration and postmodern geopolitics in *The Satanic Verses* (1988). While Herbert focuses on the spectral presence of the marginalized in Bombay, Gane's analysis of London highlights the sociospatial inequalities of the global city, where certain translocal actors—such as cosmopolitan intellectuals—are empowered, while nameless, voiceless poor migrants, especially women and children, are deprived of agency.

John McLeod (2004: 147–148) further critiques the representation of London in *The Satanic Verses*, acknowledging its status as a definitive fictional portrayal of the immigrant experience in the city, yet also noting criticisms of its authenticity due to Rushdie's privileged background. The fictional neighbourhood of Brickhall in the novel is an amalgamation of Brick Lane and Southall—areas populated by working-class immigrants. While McLeod rejects the notion that Rushdie is entirely alienated from this setting due to his privilege, he suggests that the author's own unconscious dislocation from such spaces is reflected in his anxious depiction of the Brixton riots of the 1980s. In a special issue on Postcolonial Cities, Claire Chambers and Graham Huggan (2015) engage with key debates about how such cities should be analyzed—whether primarily through cultural indicators or as part of global urban networks. They also explore shifting borders and emerging forms of marginality within postcolonial cities. Ultimately,

Chambers and Huggan valorize postcolonial cities, alongside the paradigm of postcolonialism itself, as sites of contradiction—"both modern and not, at once unwanted reminders of the past and energizing models for the future" (2015: 5).

Soja and Synekism

This chapter contributes to the ongoing debate on global cities by engaging with the work of Edward Soja to uncover alternative geohistories in Salman Rushdie's novels. Although Soja is often associated with elite global theorists, his scholarship remains in conversation with postcolonial realities, particularly through *Thirdspace: Journeys to Los Angeles and Other Real-and-Imagined Places* (1996). In this seminal work, Soja attempts to attune spatial materiality and imagination to notions of alterity and otherness by conceptualizing a radical *Third Space*, a fluid and evolving site that transcends binary reductionism. His ideas on hybridity and urban alterity also inform his alternative framework of "putting cities first"[1] in historical narratives of urban development (2008, 2010). Drawing on archaeological findings, particularly those of James Mellaart, Soja presents a geohistorical perspective where the spatial specificity of cities determines the rise and transformation of broader spatial formations.

Challenging conventional urban historiography, Soja disputes the long-standing assumption that Sumerian cities represent the first true urban centres, as posited by V. Gordon Childe in *Man Makes Himself* (1951). Instead, following Jane Jacobs's arguments in *The Economy of Cities* (1969), Soja argues that the archaeological record has largely overlooked early city formations in south-central Anatolia and the Jordan Valley, specifically the settlements of Çatal Hüyük and Jericho, which date back 9,000–10,000 years. Recognizing Çatal Hüyük as the earliest known example of urbanization not only reconfigures our understanding of when cities emerged but also necessitates a re-evaluation of what defines a city and urban culture. It further disrupts the linear progression of historical epochs—from the Palaeolithic era to industrialization—by demonstrating that the generative force of urban agglomeration, which Soja terms *synekism*, has driven the development of spatial units from early agricultural societies to city-states and eventually to modern nation-states. In this way, Soja crafts a revisionist geohistory of urban development by prioritizing cities as fundamental agents in spatial transformation.

Traditionally, urban historians and archaeologists have employed the concept of *synoecism* to examine the interdependencies of urban environments, particularly the ways in which proximity fosters cultural and political crystallization in early city-states. Soja, however, deliberately re-spells the term as *synekism* to emphasize its phonetic link to the Greek *synoikismos*, which denotes patterns of communal habitation and shared dwelling. This rearticulation allows Soja to construct a comprehensive spatial framework that captures the generative networks linking urban formations at various scales. Engaging with Charles Tilly's *Cities and States in World History* (2011), Soja highlights Çatal Hüyük as an early model of urbanization—an unwalled, weakly stratified, and possibly matriarchal settlement, characterized by the absence of centralized religious structures, sacrificial rituals, or hierarchical governance. Rather than emerging as a product of state control, this city developed organically through trade networks within a densely inhabited region, where egalitarian bands of hunters and gatherers coexisted and possibly worshipped a mother goddess. From Soja's perspective, two distinct models of urbanization emerge. The first is exemplified by the early cities of Çatal Hüyük and Jericho, which functioned independently of state authority and were shaped by inclusive, nomadic, and egalitarian cultures—potentially under matriarchal influence. The second model reflects the appropriation of cities by sovereign states, leading to hierarchical control, exclusionary policies, and the rise of a scripto-centric culture. The following section of this chapter examines how these two urban models interact across time, forming a diachronic link between the cities depicted in Rushdie's novels.

Soja, Synekism, and the Cities of Rushdie

Rushdie's novels prominently feature cities of the Global South, from the pre-Islamic city of Jahilia and the Mughal capital of Sikri to postcolonial metropolises such as Bombay and Karachi. This shift in focus disrupts the Eurocentric genealogy of urban development, which often privileges cities of the Global North as primary sites for theorizing the global city. At the same time, Rushdie's depiction of Western cities is generally filtered through the perspective of the migrant, thereby subverting the conventional parasitic relationship between the metropolis and the periphery. This chapter explores how Rushdie's fictional cities engage with Edward Soja's radical geohistory of urbanization, particularly in their spatial specificity and their role in shaping empires, nation-states, and, ultimately, the fractured identities of hybrid citizens in the post-nation. Rushdie's representation of cities demonstrates how key moments of urban formation in the Global South are deeply interconnected, marked by an ongoing contestation between the matriarchal and nomadic ethos of inclusivity and the patriarchal and statist impulse towards institutionalization and exclusion.

One of the central concerns in Rushdie's literary cartography of cities is the deconstruction of the binary between nomadism and settlement. In *The Satanic Verses* (1988), Jahilia—Rushdie's fictionalized version of seventh-century Mecca—stands at a historical juncture, on the brink of being transformed by the spread of Islam under the leadership of Mahound, a fictional counterpart of the Prophet Muhammad. Rushdie presents Jahilia as a recently formed city whose inhabitants are new converts to sedentary life from a predominantly nomadic existence. The novel portrays the city as an uneasy amalgamation of two competing forces: the established urban authority of Jahilia and the revolutionary doctrine of Islam. While these two forces stand in opposition, both integrate elements of an older, more fluid urban model shaped by the matriarchal and nomadic ethos of inclusivity while simultaneously embracing exclusionary structures characteristic of statist urbanism.

In *Joseph Anton* (2012), Rushdie acknowledges that the early history of Islam can be understood through the lens of Arabia's urbanization. He describes Islam as a response to the control and corruption of the Quraysh mercantile elite, who dominated Mecca's economy in the seventh century AD.[2] The House of the Black Stone, located at the heart of Jahilia, plays a crucial role in maintaining the city's economic and religious identity. Housing 360 idols, it serves as a sacred site that draws diverse tribes from across the region, who pay tribute to their deities during pilgrimages. However, Rushdie highlights the city's vulnerability as it faces economic decline with the waning importance of Arabian caravanserais and the rise of maritime trade. This shift places increasing pressure on Jahilia to sustain itself through religious tourism, reinforcing its reliance on a nomadic influx of outsiders. To accommodate these pilgrims and maintain the city's proto-capitalist religious economy, the authorities not only ensure their safety but also promote entertainment venues such as brothels, which function as both economic enterprises and spaces of refuge. The architecture of Jahilia, built on sand, further underscores its impermanence, symbolizing the fragility of a city whose existence is predicated on an ephemeral and shifting ecological landscape. The festival of Ibrahim, one of the key religious celebrations in Jahilia, transforms the city into a carnivalesque space where the authority of the nascent city-state is temporarily subverted. During these moments of festivity, Jahilia becomes a site of lawlessness and disorder, yet also a space of radical possibility, where non-hierarchical interactions flourish. The chief patrons of the city's religious economy are the female deities Al-Lat, Manat, and Uzza, whose human counterpart is Hind, a powerful matriarchal figure. Rushdie thus portrays Jahilia as a city where maternal and nomadic energies shape a loosely structured, inclusive urban model that remains open to otherness and difference.

Yet, beneath this inclusivity, Jahilia also possesses a rigid and stratified social structure, where social ranks are carefully maintained and movement between classes is restricted. The city is built in concentric circles, a formation reminiscent of Ernest Burgess's early twentieth-century model of urban social structures, in which the Central Business District occupies the heart of the city. In Jahilia, this central space is occupied by the House of the Black Stone and the grand palace of the city's elite ruler, Abu Simbel. The city's fortifications serve as a barrier between insiders and outsiders, signalling a shift away from its earlier nomadic ethic of inclusivity, which had been associated with the maternal instinct of sheltering outcasts and orphans. As a result, Jahilia initially resists the spread of Islam, perceiving it as a threat to its established social order.

Islam, as depicted in *The Satanic Verses*, offers an alternative urban model. Its ascetic simplicity, monotheism, and rejection of polytheistic grandeur appeal to the marginalized segments of Jahilia's population, who find themselves excluded from the city's economic and social hierarchies. While the elite benefit from the wealth generated by the religious economy, the poor are granted access to its resources only during sporadic moments of carnival and disorder. Islam, by contrast, promises a more egalitarian structure, providing refuge for outcasts such as Khalid, the water-carrier; Bilal, the freed slave; and Salman, the Persian migrant. Even Hamza, Mahound's uncle and one of the fiercest defenders of Islam, embodies the values of pre-urban nomadic tribes. Mahound himself, though born in Jahilia and a merchant by trade, exists outside the city's elite economic networks, reinforcing the idea that early Islam emerges from those excluded from urban privilege. Yet, Rushdie does not present Islam as a purely inclusive force. He suggests that its monotheistic philosophy carries within it the seeds of exclusion, as its vision of a purified space stands in direct opposition to the hybridity and multiplicity of Jahilia's religious pluralism. The destruction of Jahilia's idols marks the triumph of a patriarchal, centralized urban model over the matriarchal, decentralized ethos of the old city. This shift is reflected in the rejection of Mahound's initial revelation—the so-called "Satanic Verses"—which had accommodated the three female deities within Islam's pantheon. The erasure of this revelation from the written Quran parallels the replacement of Jahilia's pluralistic urbanism with a rigid, monolithic urban culture sustained by written scripture and hierarchical governance.

Despite the dominance of the new Islamic order, an alternative urban model briefly emerges within Jahilia itself: the brothel known as *The Curtain*. Here, the satirist and anti-prophet Baal constructs a subversive counter-city. The brothel functions as a parallel sacred space, centred around the Fountain of Love, which serves as a parody of the House of the Black Stone. Just as pilgrims in Mecca circumambulate the Kaaba, Baal's clients form a queue in concentric circles around the Fountain of Love, reenacting the sacred pilgrimage in a profane and irreverent manner. Within *The Curtain*, Baal assumes the role of prophet, and the twelve prostitutes symbolize Mahound's twelve wives, further subverting the sanctity of the Islamic city.

This parody of the sacred order is short-lived. The alternative city of *The Curtain* is ultimately crushed by Mahound's forces, and all those involved in its blasphemous drama are executed. In this final moment, Rushdie brings the tension between Jahilia's two competing urban models to a dramatic close, affirming the continuous struggle between the inclusive, chaotic urbanism of the nomadic past and the exclusionary, hierarchical structures of the state-controlled city.

The next significant moment of city-formation captured in Rushdie's novels unfolds in early sixteenth-century Florence and Sikri, as well as in fourteenth-century Vijayanagar (later Bisnaga). These cities, both powerful in their time, represent distinct yet intersecting models of urban existence. Sikri emerges as a city built from nothing, a grand manifestation of an absolute monarch's vision, while Florence thrives under the oligarchic rule of the Medici family. Echoing the tensions seen in Jahilia, these cities embody two competing models of urban life: one that is loose, matriarchal, nomadic, and inclusive, and another that is statist, patriarchal, rigidly hierarchical, and governed by exclusionary politics. These models engage in a subtle yet decisive contest for dominance, each reflecting and resisting the forces shaping their histories.

Florence and Sikri, despite their geographical and political differences, share a fundamental contradiction in their existence. Sikri, built as a seemingly permanent dwelling with Akbar's grand fort at its centre—a symbol of absolute authority—retains an inherent transience, much like Jahilia, the city of sand. The Mughal monarchs themselves had led a semi-nomadic existence only a few generations prior, mirroring the transition of Arabic tribes from a nomadic to a city-dwelling life in Jahilia. This interplay of permanence and impermanence is further reinforced through the figure of Qara Qoz, the Mughal princess who is reconstructed from the forgotten past through Niccolò Vespucci's tales and Akbar's imagination. In a moment of temporal fluidity, where past and future fold into one another, Qara Qoz dreams of Sikri as a projection of what is to come. In her vision, the temporary "canopies and cupolas" of Babur's tents—symbols of the Mughal dynasty's nomadic origins—solidify into the permanence of red sandstone palaces, signifying the establishment of Sikri.

Yet, like all mirage-like cities in Rushdie's narratives, Sikri's grandeur is short-lived. When its vital water source, the "golden life-giving lake" (2008: 344), dries up, Akbar abandons the city. However, his concern is not merely the loss of Sikri as a physical space but the symbolic weight of Niccolò Vespucci's curse, which foresees the decline of the Mughal Empire itself. Vespucci, once embraced by Akbar as the "Mughal of Love"—an honorary title given in an attempt to integrate the foreigner within Mughal identity based on imagined fraternal bonds rather than biological lineage—is ultimately cast out. His banishment stems from his role as a storyteller, a spinner of licentious tales that threaten the stability of the city's narrative order.

Florence, in both Rushdie's novels and historical reality, appears more enduring than Sikri, yet it too carries the fluidity of a dreamed-up city. When Akbar envisions Florence through Niccolò Vespucci's stories, he simultaneously exoticizes it and reconstructs it in the image of the East—an ironic reversal of the Orientalist gaze. Rushdie's Florence, then, becomes a space of narrative inversion, where the West is subjected to the same kind of myth-making that the East has historically endured (2008: 329–330). Nicole Weickgenannt Thiara (2011) describes Florence and Sikri as "enabling" spaces—cities that, by opening themselves to the enchantment of a woman (Qara Qoz), acquire a cosmopolitan and dynamic character that makes them more alike than their historical realities might suggest.

This chapter argues that it is the openness of both Florence and Sikri to enchantment—particularly to the transformative presence of the nomadic Mughal princess Qara Qoz—that aligns them with matriarchal and fluid energies, resisting the rigid, imperial histories of colonial modernity. Rather than subscribing to a civilizing mission that seeks to assimilate or dominate, these cities momentarily embrace a different vision—one where magic and humanism intersect, where feminine enchantment and Renaissance secularism merge to create a more egalitarian urban space. Within this framework, feminine spells and charms do not induce fear or superstition but instead foster a unity of civilizations, enabling inclusive socio-spatial practices that transcend the binary of East and West.

However, this openness to enchantment is ultimately rejected by both cities. Akbar dismisses the phantasmal conclusion of Qara Qoz's tale as told by Niccolò Vespucci, rejecting its improbable elements—particularly the notion of Qara Qoz halting time in the Mundus Novus, the New World. Instead, he replaces it with a darker, more "realistic" ending, where Niccolò Vespucci is revealed to be the incestuous offspring of Ago Vespucci and his daughter with Qara Qoz. Similarly, Florence turns against the miracles of Qara Qoz, suppressing the subversive and seductive power of feminine energy by branding it as witchcraft. The rejection of enchantment leads to the decline of both cities: Sikri's existence ends with its physical abandonment, while Florence loses its prominence as the river Arno itself metaphorically "dries up" in response to the city's closing off from the outsider, the nomadic, and the matriarchal. Thus, Florence and Sikri, despite their initial openness to magic, imagination, and hybridity, ultimately succumb to the same forces that define the imperial histories they momentarily sought to transcend. They are cities caught in the eternal cycle of creation and destruction, a cycle that Rushdie repeatedly explores in his literary cityscapes.

In *Victory City* (2023), Salman Rushdie envisions a radically different kind of city from those depicted in his earlier works. Unlike Jahilia, Sikri, or Florence—where power is contested between patriarchal, statist forces and nomadic, matriarchal energies—Bisnaga emerges as a feminist utopia, a city shaped by the vision of a woman and founded on principles of equality, wisdom, and cultural flourishing. While Rushdie's earlier cities exist in a state of tension, caught between the forces of enchantment and rigid social hierarchies, Bisnaga begins as a place of balance, a realm where imagination, justice, and governance are interwoven. However, as history has shown time and again, utopias are precarious, vulnerable to the pressures of ambition, power struggles, and the inexorable return of patriarchal dominance. At the heart of the novel is Pampa Kampana, an orphaned girl who witnesses firsthand the horrors of war, destruction, and the erasure of cultures. Chosen by the goddess Parvati as a vessel for divine power, she is tasked with creating a new world—a society where women hold positions of influence, where wisdom and justice prevail over brute force, and where history is rewritten to accommodate the dreams of the marginalized rather than the ambitions of conquerors. From a handful of seeds, Pampa whispers Bisnaga into existence, conjuring an entire civilization through the power of words. Her act of creation is not merely political or magical but deeply symbolic: it represents an alternative history, a defiant rejection of the rigid, exclusionary cities that have dominated historical narratives.

Bisnaga, meaning "Victory City," flourishes under Pampa's guidance. Unlike the imperial ambitions of the Mughals in Sikri or the oligarchic rule of the Medici in Florence, Bisnaga is imagined as a city of inclusivity, where power is shared rather than hoarded, and where women are not confined to the margins of history but stand at its centre. Unlike the fleeting mirage of Jahilia, which is ultimately consumed by the forces of orthodoxy, Bisnaga seems, for a time, to be a lasting vision—proof that an alternative form of civilization is possible. Its foundations, unlike those of earlier cities in Rushdie's works, are built not on conquest or exclusion but on storytelling, enchantment, and a reimagining of history itself.

Yet, as time passes, the forces that have historically dismantled such dreams begin to encroach upon Bisnaga's utopia. Patriarchy, political ambition, and human frailty seep into the city's foundations, eroding the radical vision upon which it was built. Though Pampa Kampana is its creator, its guardian, and its spiritual force, she finds herself increasingly marginalized as power shifts into the hands of men who seek to reshape Bisnaga according to their own desires. The city that once symbolized possibility becomes a battleground of competing ideologies, a site of betrayal and disillusionment. Pampa, once worshipped as a goddess and revered as a leader, is eventually cast out of the very city she brought into existence. Her exile is not merely a political fall from grace but a symbolic unravelling of her vision—without her presence, Bisnaga begins to lose its essence, its identity dissolving into the familiar patterns of history. In her final years, she goes blind, a devastating loss of sight that mirrors the fading of her dream. Her blindness is more than a physical affliction; it represents the erasure of her utopia, the inevitability of history's cycles, where radical dreams are repeatedly suppressed by the weight of entrenched power structures.

Bisnaga, once a beacon of matriarchal governance and cultural brilliance, succumbs to the same fate as other grand cities before it. The ideals upon which it was built—equality, justice, and a rejection of patriarchal domination—are gradually replaced by ambition, control, and the familiar constraints of historical precedent. Like Sikri, which is abandoned when its water source runs dry, and Florence, which loses its prominence when it closes itself off to the nomadic and the foreign, Bisnaga ultimately crumbles under the weight of its own contradictions. Yet, *Victory City* is not merely a lament for a lost civilization. Rushdie's novel is a meditation on the power of storytelling, on the ways in which history is shaped not only by victors but by those who dare to imagine alternatives. Though Bisnaga falls, its memory persists through the tales that survive, through the echoes of Pampa Kampana's whispered words. While Bisnaga may be lost, its story remains— a testament to the resilience of those who dare to dream of a different world.

The penultimate moment of city-formation in Rushdie's novels unfolds in his depiction of postcolonial Bombay and Karachi. In works such as *Midnight's Children* (1981), *The Satanic Verses* (1988), *The Moor's Last Sigh* (1995), and *The Ground Beneath Her Feet* (1999), Bombay from the 1950s to the 1980s emerges as a vibrant, hybrid metropolis shaped by migration and sustained by an indigenous, grassroots cosmopolitanism. This form of cosmopolitanism is distinct from the Eurocentric ideals of inclusivity rooted in Renaissance humanism or Enlightenment thought, and it does not stem from the consumer-driven multiculturalism of contemporary globalization. Nor can it be dismissed as a nostalgic, exoticized representation of a "Third World Cosmopolitan" (Brennan, 1989) catering to Western literary markets.

Bombay's cosmopolitan ethos also resists the statist model of "Unity in Diversity" promoted by post-independence India under Nehruvian socialism. While this vision sought to construct a secular and inclusive nation, it was ultimately marked by a tendency towards centralization, imposing unity from above rather than allowing it to emerge organically from the lived spaces of diverse communities. In Rushdie's novels, Bombay's identity is deeply intertwined with the private, domestic sphere—represented through homes that serve as microcosms of the city itself. Despite their patriarchal structures, these homes derive their warmth and inclusivity from everyday female rituals and gossip, shaping them into dynamic, open spaces. This duality is evident in the homes of the city's elite, such as Aurora Zogoiby's coterie in *The Moor's Last Sigh* (1995) and *The Ground Beneath Her Feet* (1999), as well as in the precarious yet welcoming spaces inhabited by figures like Saleem Sinai in *Midnight's Children* (1981). Saleem, an orphan of mixed European and subaltern Indian descent, embodies the contradictions of postcolonial Bombay—a city both inclusive and fragmented, both unified and chaotic.

In contrast, Rushdie's portrayal of Karachi in *Midnight's Children* (1981) and *Shame* (1983) presents a city deeply entangled in the contradictions of postcolonial modernity. As the face of Pakistan's urban modernity, Karachi serves as a symbol of progress, yet it remains haunted by the enduring influence of tribal allegiances and patriarchal traditions. The novel *Shame* (1983) juxtaposes Karachi with the Mohenjo estate of Iskander Harappa and the Daro estate of Little Mir in Sindh, evoking the ancient cities of Mohenjo-Daro and Harappa. This allusion reinforces the historical depth of Pakistan's hinterlands, which exist outside the temporal framework of postcolonial modernity imposed by the nation-state. While Karachi presents itself as a forward-looking metropolis, its public sphere remains a male-dominated space of political and sexual power, exemplified by figures like Iskander Harappa and Omar Khayyam. Women, such as Rani Harappa, are relegated to the oppressive confines of ancestral homes, reinforcing the exclusionary nature of Karachi's modernity. However, Rushdie subverts this male hegemony through the character of Tai Bibi, the "oldest whore in the world," whom Saleem tracks down using his heightened sense of smell in *Midnight's Children* (1981). Her presence suggests the persistence of female agency operating beneath the surface of Karachi's male-centric order.

While Bombay, in Rushdie's vision, represents an alternative model of a nomadic, matriarchal city, this ideal remains compromised by the city's elitist representation, which largely overlooks the realities of urban poverty and the struggles of the marginalized. Conversely, Karachi, despite its claim to modernity, ultimately excludes women and the subaltern from its emancipatory potential. This exclusion finds its most extreme expression in *Shame* (1983) through Sufiya Zinobia, the mentally challenged daughter of Raza Hyder, whose uncontrollable rage leads her to commit violent homicides. Her psychotic episodes, though appearing as acts of cathartic violence, ultimately create a spectacle of destruction rather than a space for cohabitation and agency. Thus, Karachi's modernity remains fundamentally limited, promising inclusivity but ultimately reinforcing patriarchal hierarchies.

Paradoxically, while Karachi's urban modernity excludes women and the subaltern, Bombay's encounter with global modernity leads to a regressive, nativist politics. The rise of the Shiv Sena in the 1990s, foreshadowed in the farcical language marchers' riot of the 1950s in *Midnight's Children* (1981), marks a shift towards ethnic violence and exclusionary urban politics. By targeting migrants—particularly non-Hindus and non-Marathi speakers— Shiv Sena enforces a patriarchal and statist model of the city that mirrors the exclusionary dynamics of Karachi. In Rushdie's portrayal, these forces threaten to dismantle the cosmopolitan, hybrid city that Bombay once represented, replacing it with an authoritarian, intolerant urban landscape.

The final moment of city-formation in Rushdie's novels unfolds in the global North, where cities are shaped by the forces of transnational capital and migration in an era of "time-space compression." In this landscape, traditional notions of the city as a territorially bounded unit dissolve, giving rise to fluid, amorphous networks of flows. However, these flows are not solely dictated by corporate globalization; they are also shaped by the movement of postcolonial migrants who challenge and redefine urban spaces. In *The Satanic Verses* (1988), London's transterritoriality is facilitated by air travel and mass media, creating a spectral cityscape where migrant histories intertwine with the metropolis's present, destabilizing its spatiotemporal axis.

Rushdie's portrayal of New York and Los Angeles similarly reconfigures these cities through the perspective of the migrant. In *Shalimar the Clown* (2005), Los Angeles—a city typically associated with spectacle and entertainment—is linked to the global network of terrorism through the assassination of Max Ophuls by Shalimar. This act of violence collapses the distance between the micro-level domestic tragedies of Kashmir and the large-scale geopolitics of global terror, illustrating how violence in the global South reverberates through the metropolises of the West. Similarly, *Fury* (2001) presents New York as a city consumed by dematerialized global capital, where hyperreality is orchestrated through cyberculture and media spectacle. The character Malik Solanka, creator of the celebrity doll Little Brain, navigates a world where reality is increasingly shaped by digital consumption, while the novel's subplots extend this virtual reality to the postcolonial Lilliput-Blefuscu Island (a stand-in for Fiji), where insurgent leader Babur appropriates cyber-fiction for his own revolutionary cause. Through these global cityscapes, Rushdie presents a vision of the postmetropolis as a site of constant deterritorialization and reterritorialization. While transnational capital reinforces new hegemonies of controlled societies, alternative flows—generated by postcolonial migrants—carve out spaces of resistance. As Castells notes, these migrants produce "alternative spaces of flows based on spaces of places," thereby challenging the dominance of corporate globalization. However, these urban landscapes are also sites of violence, where racial riots, serial killers, and acts of rage mark the contested terrain of the migrant's struggle. In these dystopian spaces, migrants are both victims and agents of transformation, asserting their right to the city by reshaping it in their own image. Ultimately, Rushdie's cities exist in a state of perpetual flux, where the patriarchal, statist city is continuously destabilized by the forces of migration, hybridity, and nomadic existence. This ongoing process of deterritorialization and reterritorialization dissolves rigid oppositions, giving rise to hybrid, cyborg-like cities—urban spaces that are never fully formed but are always in the process of becoming.

Conclusion

Rushdie's portrayal of cities offers a compelling lens through which to navigate postcolonial and global conflicts, as he maps out non-hierarchical, networked urban formations that predate and extend beyond the British colonial moment. His narratives highlight how cities serve as dynamic contact zones where global flows intersect with local realities, collapsing traditional boundaries between the home and the world. This perspective aligns with Soja's call to "putting cities first," (2003) positioning urban spaces as the primary scale for understanding social, economic, and political transformations. Both Rushdie, as a novelist, and Soja, as a social theorist, trace the generative impulse of urban agglomeration to early globalization, challenging the dominant discourse that frames contemporary urban networks solely through the transnational nodes of the post-Fordist economy. Rushdie's literary cartography excavates alternative connections between cities that have been marginalized in discussions of twenty-first-century global metropolises. His novels contextualize these networks not only through imaginative urban landscapes but also within the realpolitik of key historical moments in the Global South. The various phases of urban formation in Rushdie's works offer glimpses into the potential of cities in the Global South as spaces of refuge, hybridity, and maternal inclusivity. These stand in contrast to the exclusionary, institutionalized, and statist forces that seek to control them. This tension—between the fluid, nomadic city and the rigid, hierarchical one—creates a throughline across Rushdie's urban narratives, linking different moments of synekism while preserving traces of resistance. In doing so, his novels open pathways for reimagining contemporary global urbanism as an evolving space of contestation, transformation, and possibility.

Notes

1 Gordon Childe's classical work *Man Makes Himself* (1951) authoritatively illustrates how society evolved from the Palaeolithic (stone) to the Neolithic (agriculture) and then to the Urban and Industrial age. According to him, the break from the Neolithic to the Urban age occurred around 6000 years ago as the first true cities evolved in Mesopotamia along the fertile alluvial plain of Tigris and Euphrates as a result of the production of agricultural surplus. Eventually,

this impulse of city-formation spread to the West over thousands of centuries culminating in the advanced city-states of the Greeks and Romans. The transition to the Urban age was marked by expansion in agricultural infrastructure as well as increasing centralization of authority, which was reflected in the city's built environment with the city being walled for heightened security and its centre marked by walled palaces and temples. The transition also produced the elaborate stratification of society into a rapidly stringent class structure and the related emergence of a complex and hierarchized political system. Finally, one needs to mention the emergence of writing technology engendering and sustaining the urban culture in this context.

2 Rushdie was a student of history at Cambridge University, and he mentions in *Joseph Anton* (2012) that the history of early Islam had fascinated him immensely even as a young undergraduate student. It may be understood (Rushdie also mentions his sources in *Joseph Anton* [2012]) that Rushdie's account of the early Mecca is based on Islamic sources such as Hadith of Ibn Ishaq, Al Tabari, etc. and on Western scholarly sources such as W. Montgomery Watt, Maxime Rodinson's accounts of the early life of Mohammed in Mecca. Many of Rushdie's sources have been refuted and modified in the recent scholarship on Mecca during the seventh century AD; particular mention must be made of Patricia Crone's *Meccan Trade and the Rise of Islam* (1987) where she clearly opposes the established notion (primarily Watt's account of Mecca during Mohammed's time by decoding the historical evidences from within the Quran) that Mecca was the central point of large-scale Arabian incense trade or the focal point of Arabia's trade with Syria, Egypt, Yemen, Iraq or Ethiopia. She also refutes the widely held idea that the Quraysh tribe controlled huge trade inflows in Arabia and that Mecca was the centre of pilgrimages, fairs and carnivals, and sanctuaries. However, the portrayal of Jahilia in *The Satanic Verses* (1988) is based on these traditional sources of understanding the history and sociology of early Islam.

4

BOMBAY IN SALMAN RUSHDIE'S NOVELS

A Study from Alternative Global Perspective

Introduction

> To understand just one life, you have to swallow the world. I told you
> that the world was too much with me; but in fact, the reverse is true. The
> world is not in my body. It is on me, it is outside me, it has crushed me
> beneath it … And Bombay is the heart of it all. A city built by foreigners
> upon reclaimed land, Bombay was central, had always been so, to my
> story. Bombay, where my grandfather came to study, where my father met
> my mother, where I was born … A city built on a wish, a dream, a fantasy.
> (*Midnight's Children* 1981)

Bombay, the city where Salman Rushdie spent his formative years, fea-
tures prominently in four of his major novels: *Midnight's Children (1981)*,
The Satanic Verses (1988), *The Moor's Last Sigh (1995)*, *and The Ground
Beneath Her Feet (1999)*. Although traditional Rushdie scholarship has
paid limited attention to his portrayal of cities, the subject has increasingly attracted critical interest in recent years. Contemporary studies have
approached Bombay through various lenses: as a "lettered city" (Khanna,
2011), as artists' material (Khanna, 2006), as a mirror reconstituting
London through catoptric imagery in *The Satanic Verses* (Parashkevova,
2007), or as Rushdie's "only ideal city," which, rather than reflecting a utopian postcolonial promise, ultimately reveals the disillusionment and "unre-
alizable dreams of the postcolonial citizen" (Upstone, 2009: 87). However,
these literary interpretations often overlook the material and spatial dimensions of Bombay that permeate Rushdie's fiction. Such approaches tend to
obscure the city as a real-imagined, lived space—what Henri Lefebvre (1991)
describes as "representational space" and Edward Soja (1996) terms "third

DOI: 10.4324/9781003106180-4

space." In an increasingly placeless globalized world, the recovery of lived space—whether at the micro level of the body or the macro level of communities—has become a vital concern for contemporary spatial theorists. The debate surrounding "place" and "placelessness," which gained prominence with the onset of globalization, can be traced back to the work of humanistic geographers in the 1970s. In *Place and Placelessness* (1976), Edward Relph distinguishes between two modes of experiencing place. The "authentic" mode arises from what he calls "existential insideness," characterized by a sense of belonging and emotional rootedness. In contrast, the "inauthentic" experience, or "existential outsideness," is marked by feelings of alienation and detachment. For Relph, placelessness denotes the erosion of place through mass-produced environments and the dominance of technological efficiency—what he refers to as "kitsch" and "technique." Similarly, Yi-Fu Tuan's (1974) concept of *topophilia*—a strong affective bond with place—serves as a counterforce against the homogenizing effects of globalization.

While these early studies raise important concerns about the displacement and standardization of place under global capitalism, they often adopt a romanticized and static conception of place, overlooking its dynamic, processual nature. In this sense, their approaches, though foundational in emphasizing the qualitative and experiential aspects of place during the quantitative turn in geography, fall short of a *critical* understanding of place. By contrast, geographers influenced by Henri Lefebvre—such as David Harvey and Doreen Massey—offer more nuanced frameworks. They reconceptualize place not as fixed or pure but as shaped by socio-spatial processes and embedded in global interconnections. Similarly, Manuel Castells (1989), in his analysis of the informational economy, differentiates between the "space of places" and the "space of flows." Yet, Castells also acknowledges the capacity of local actors to reassert place through grassroots urban movements, even as he warns that these efforts can turn into reactionary, territorially bounded responses. Ultimately, he advocates for "alternative spaces of flows" that remain grounded in the materiality and specificity of place. The chapter also seeks to demonstrate that the nuances of Rushdie's portrayal of Bombay align with Doreen Massey's concept of a "global sense of place" (1994)—a radical reimagining of place as both uniquely characterized and inherently dynamic. This perspective resists the essentializing or tribalizing of place by acknowledging its fluid nature as both process and product, thereby offering a way to navigate the crisis of identity and community brought about by the forces of global capitalism.

Bombay as Lived Space

This chapter argues that Rushdie's depiction of Bombay, particularly through the motif of land reclamation, offers a powerful lens into the city's lived experience. His portrayal articulates a progressive, global sense of place—one that neither collapses into nostalgic nativism nor dissolves into abstract, deterritorialized globalism. Land reclamation, as depicted in Rushdie's Bombay novels, serves as a microcosm of his broader treatment of the city. In Rushdie's fictional world, Bombay emerges as a dynamic "process"—a space of constant flux, precariously balanced between movement and stillness, permanence and transience. It is a migrant's city, a place of ephemeral homes that are at once nurturing and ominous. Despite its instability, Bombay retains a distinctive character, marked by what Arjun Appadurai describes as a cosmopolitanism from below—a cultural ethos grounded in coexistence, hybridity, and the everyday mingling of diverse lives. As Appadurai (2011: n.p.) asserts,

> the cosmopolitanism in Mumbai is rarely identified with self-cultivation, universalism, or with the ideals of globalism with which it is historically linked in Enlightenment Europe. Rather, it is primarily identified with cultural co-existence, the positive valuation of mixture and intercultural contact, the refusal of monoculturalism as a governing value, and a strong sense of the inherent virtues of rubbing shoulders with those who speak other languages, eat other foods, worship other gods, and wear their clothes differently.

This perspective highlights a form of cosmopolitanism rooted not in abstract ideals but in the lived, everyday practices of pluralism and proximity that define the city's social fabric.

In Rushdie's novels, episodes surrounding land-reclamation in Bombay reveal that space is not merely a passive backdrop but a material construct shaped through socio-spatial practices and the contestation of multiple interests—those of the city's inhabitants and those of external, often impersonal forces. In a globalized context, these external forces increasingly take the form of corporatized capital, justified by the language of development and modernity that swiftly encroaches upon the lived spaces of the Global South. Rushdie's depiction of Bombay through the lens of land-reclamation offers insight into this lived, pluralistic space—rendering it as a dynamic product rather than a fixed entity, and positioning it in opposition to the top-down spatial restructuring undertaken by state-sponsored capitalist development throughout the latter half of the twentieth century.

However, Rushdie is equally critical of the ethnic politics of groups like Shiv Sena, whose imagination of Bombay as an exclusively Marathi homeland constitutes a reactionary force against the city's inherent diversity. Shiv Sena, a regional political party based in Maharashtra, was founded by Bal Thackeray in 1966 and is rooted in the ideology of asserting

Maharashtra—and particularly Mumbai—as the rightful domain of the Marathi people. With Shiv Sena's rise to power in the state, the city of Bombay was officially renamed Mumbai in 1995. In Rushdie's Bombay novels, this renaming signifies more than a linguistic or administrative shift; it marks a transformation in the very character of the city—from a vibrant, cosmopolitan hub to one increasingly defined by parochialism, communal tensions, and the growing influence of underworld networks. The change reflects a broader cultural and political reorientation, as the city's pluralistic ethos gives way to exclusionary identity politics and sectarian strife. These identity-based narratives, which gain momentum in the context of a rapidly globalizing metropolis, undermine the hybrid and fluid character of the city that Rushdie so vividly portrays. This chapter argues that Rushdie's nuanced representation of Bombay resonates with Doreen Massey's concept of a "global sense of place" (1994)—a radical approach that understands place as a constellation of relations and processes, shaped by mobility and interaction, rather than as static or essentialist. By embracing this vision, Rushdie resists both the homogenizing forces of global capital and the tribalizing tendencies of nativist politics, offering instead a model of place rooted in multiplicity, openness, and critical engagement with modernity.

Rushdie's portrayal of Bombay has often been interpreted through the lens of diasporic place-making, frequently reduced to a deterritorialized landscape shaped by nostalgia and memory. Bill Ashcroft's insights into the spatial practices of diasporic communities are particularly relevant here. He argues that for diasporic peoples, "place" may no longer refer to a concrete geographical location, as the intrinsic connection between identity and physical space may have been irrevocably severed (Ashcroft, 2001: 125). Instead, belonging becomes embedded in family, community, cultural symbols, and shared experiences, forming what Ashcroft calls a "deterritorialized symbol" of home—often steeped in nostalgia and collective memory. Rushdie's own comment in *Imaginary Homelands* (1992) reflects the diasporic impulse to recreate a lost homeland through fiction. He notes, "Our physical alienation from India almost inevitably means that we will not be able to reclaim precisely the thing that was lost... we will in short create fictions, not actual cities or villages but invisible ones, imaginary homelands" (1992: 2). However, this chapter challenges the idea that Bombay in Rushdie's fiction exists only as a nostalgic or symbolic space. While memory undoubtedly plays a key role in his narratives, Rushdie's Bombay is not merely a "transparent" mindscape divorced from material immediacy. Instead, it offers tangible access to the city as a "lived space," in Henri Lefebvre's (1991) and Edward Soja's (1996) sense—a dynamic, real-imagined site shaped by socio-spatial practices. Despite the absence of descriptive realism, Rushdie recreates a sense of territoriality and neighbourhood through the socio-spatial rhythms of everyday life. The city emerges not just as a setting but as a product of its inhabitants' interactions and experiences. Therefore, even though Rushdie's reconstruction of Bombay may be mediated by memory, it resonates strongly with readers familiar with the city's textures, neighbourhoods, and temporalities.

Yet, Rushdie's portrayal is not wholly egalitarian. The elite enclaves of South Bombay, featured prominently in his novels, are depicted as fantastical realms detached from the city's larger urban realities. Zeeny Vakil's remark in *The Satanic Verses* that these neighbourhoods resemble "Wonderland, Peristan, Never Never, Oz" (Rushdie, 1988: 59) underscores their sanitized depiction—largely untouched by poverty, overcrowding, or political chaos. Rushdie's Bombay, populated by cosmopolitan elites—wealthy Parsis, Kashmiri Muslims, Cochin Jews, and business magnates—is shaped by privilege. Gyan Prakash, in *Mumbai Fables* (2011), reminds us that this celebration of Bombay as a city of dreams overlooks its long history of inequality and exploitation, rooted in its origins as a colonial port. For instance, while Rushdie eulogizes the city's Art Deco architecture as a symbol of Bombay's modernization, he overlooks its connection to industrial modernity and the commodification of urban aesthetics during the interwar period (2011: 102–103). However, Rushdie offsets this by reasserting the city as a space of appropriation—where inhabitants reinterpret the "abstract" spaces imposed by planners, developers, and the state. He becomes what Lefebvre might call a "rhythmanalyst"—a listener to the city's multiple temporalities, someone who perceives its smells, sounds, and social rhythms, capturing Bombay as a living, breathing entity rather than a product of capitalist design. It is through the motif of land-reclamation that Rushdie most powerfully illustrates the interplay between imagined and lived space.

Land-Reclamation in Bombay and Rushdie's Global Sense of Place

Bombay's very formation is rooted in colonial-era land-reclamation—a social and physical engineering project that transformed seven islands (Colaba, Little Colaba, Bombay, Mazagaon, Worli, Parel, and Mahim) into a continuous landmass. Initiated by the British in the eighteenth and nineteenth centuries, this transformation continued into the twentieth century, shaping Bombay's geography and its socio-economic hierarchies. David Harvey (1993) has noted that places, like time and space, are shaped by speculative capitalist investments. Gyan Prakash echoes this idea in his critique of the Backbay land-reclamation projects in *Mumbai Fables*. He characterizes these projects as an effort to "rob the sea for the rich" (2011: 80)—to carve out elite residential zones for Bombay's affluent classes. Launched in earnest under Governor Sir George Lloyd in the early twentieth century, the Backbay project was marketed as a remedy for the city's housing crisis. Yet the plan was deeply flawed. Engineer Sir George Buchanan misjudged its scale and cost, while architect W.R. Davidge's grandiose vision remained irrelevant to the city's pressing needs. The project ultimately collapsed under accusations of corruption and inefficiency.

Despite this failure, the colonial administration continued its ambitions to reshape Bombay's coastline. Marine Drive—lined with Art Deco buildings—emerged in the 1930s as a symbol of elite urbanism. The postcolonial era saw a reprise of this developmental impulse. The 1970s witnessed renewed Backbay reclamation efforts that mirrored earlier fiascos. Urban visionaries like Charles Correa, Shirish Patel, and Pravina Mehta advocated for decentralization through the creation of Navi Mumbai (New Bombay), supported by CIDCO. Yet government preference for developing the lucrative north-south axis—including Marine Drive and Cuffe Parade—undermined the eastward expansion. Once again, corruption, poor planning, and profiteering plagued the project. The scandal culminated in a public interest petition and the resignation of Chief Minister V.P. Naik. Ironically, the newly developed Nariman Point—built on reclaimed land—became emblematic of both progress and the exclusionary logic of postcolonial development.

Rushdie's reflections in *Imaginary Homelands* reinforce the metaphorical power of land-reclamation: "Bombay is a city built by foreigners upon reclaimed land" (1992: 10). Speaking to Günter Grass, Rushdie describes his need to reclaim the city imaginatively, as the physical city of his childhood had been effaced by modernization. He draws a powerful parallel between Bombay's literal reclamation from the sea and his own literary effort to retrieve it from memory:

> The city that I remember … was knocked down and replaced by high-rise buildings, like concrete tombstones … I felt I had to go through a similar process of land-reclamation to get the city back for myself.
>
> *(Reder, 2000: 72)*

Rushdie's novels consistently return to the affluent neighbourhoods born of reclamation—Malabar Hill, Marine Drive, Cuffe Parade, and Apollo Bunder. These spaces feature prominently in *Midnight's Children*, *The Satanic Verses*, *The Moor's Last Sigh*, and *The Ground Beneath Her Feet*. Whether it is Methwold Estate, Elephanta, Scandal Point, or Everest Villa, these spaces embody the paradox of reclaimed land: simultaneously artificial and deeply lived, symbols of both colonial legacy and postcolonial transformation. Rushdie's metaphor of the "reverse Atlantis" (1995: 185)— land rising from the sea—captures Bombay's dual nature as both utopia and dystopia. It reflects a city constantly in flux, precariously balanced between movement and stasis, fantasy and decay. By anchoring his narratives in the specific histories of land-reclamation, Rushdie maps Bombay not merely as a fictional homeland but as a layered, lived space—a palimpsest shaped by colonial ambition, capitalist restructuring, and everyday resistance. His sense of place aligns with Doreen Massey's concept of a "global sense of place" (1994)—a vision of place as relational, open, and processual—capable of accommodating multiplicity without retreating into nostalgia or essentialism.

In *Midnight's Children*, Salman Rushdie traces the birth of Bombay from the arrival of the Koli fishermen to its colonization and transformation. He recounts the city's evolution from a fishing settlement to a colonial port, named "Bom Bahia" by the Portuguese, and ultimately handed over to the British as part of Catherine Braganza's dowry to Charles II. This marks the beginning of rapid urban transformation, as Rushdie describes: "off they [the British] went, with their Fort and land-reclamation, before you could blink there was a city here." Rushdie's critique of land-reclamation projects is embodied in the character of Dr Narlikar, whose ambitious plan to reclaim land from the sea reflects the modernist fantasy of rational city planning and population control. Narlikar proposes using tetrapods to create new land, symbolizing a techno-utopian response to Bombay's overcrowding. However, the project is thwarted by traditional forces, as beggar women worship the tetrapods as Shiva-lingams, transforming the symbols of sterile modernity into objects of fertility. The project ends in failure when Dr Narlikar is killed during a protest, illustrating a violent clash between rationalist development and the lived, instinctual space of the city. Ironically, the project later succeeds under the enterprising Narlikar women, who capitalize on the reclaimed land to build the high-rises of Malabar Hill, signalling the city's shift from historical charm to capitalist homogenization. Saleem Sinai's return to Bombay in the 1970s reveals a city transformed beyond recognition. The landmarks of his childhood are replaced by towering pink obelisks, symbols of modern real estate development. His disillusionment with the city reflects Rushdie's broader critique: the failure of 1950s modernization gives way to the lifeless uniformity of the 1970s urban landscape. In *The Moor's Last Sigh*, Rushdie uses the metaphor of the palimpsest to evoke Bombay's layered complexity. Aurora Zogoiby's palimpsestic paintings mirror the city, where "worlds collide, flow in and out of one another." This metaphor captures the fluidity of Bombay's space, again complicated by land-reclamation. Abraham Zogoiby, Moraes' father, is involved in a corrupt land development scheme in the Backbay area. Collaborating with municipal officials, he manipulates land values and subverts regulations to maximize profit, illustrating the entanglement of capital, crime, and governance in urban planning. This nexus disenfranchises migrant labourers and exacerbates socio-spatial inequality. The criminalization of space through capitalist expansion echoes the violent imposition of abstract, homogenizing space over the city's lived realities.

Particularly, in *The Ground Beneath Her Feet*, Rushdie masterfully illustrates his nuanced understanding of the "unsolidity of the solid ground" (54). The novel is connected by a series of earthquakes, the ultimate one leads to Vina Apsara's disappearance underground, reinforcing the tragedy of Orpheus/Eurydice myth, around which the novel is built. In this novel Rushdie uses "geology as metaphor" (1999: 203)—the physical rupturing of the "natural space" becoming a commentary on not only the mythic metatext of the novel but also the "social space" that Rushdie intends to investigate in this novel. Therefore, unsurprisingly Rushdie, in this novel, fleshes out his concerns regarding the land-reclamation very clearly. Talking about Bombay in the 1960s, the narrator says "in those days of upheaval the ground itself seemed uncertain, the physical land, seemed to cry out for reconstruction" (1999: 60). Rai's father, V.V. Merchant, being an "architect, excavator and local historian," obsesses with the pre-history of the city and digs deep in to "the underground memory of the city the British built" so that he could find "fixity in knowledge, seeking solid ground beneath the shifting sands of the age" (1999: 60). Rai's mother, Ameer Merchant is an "entrepreneur, a developer" whose dream is to build "mansions fit for God, but men will live in them" (1999: 60). Ultimately, her dream of "Cuffescrapers," the high-rises of the Cuffe Parade materializes, but its Apollonian energy is usurped by the devious scheming of the chief villain of the Bombay part of the novel—Piloo Doodhwala. Doodhwala's plan of "More Cuffe ... phor our Parade" (1999: 165) reflects the evil nexus of the developers and the government during the Backbay reclamation and eventually results in falling apart of the marriage of Rai's parents. After Ameer Merchant's untimely death, Rai and his father go to visit the construction site in Cuffe Parade. The description is eloquent:

> The long process of levelling and the reclamation was almost complete. The villas, promenade and mangrove forest was long gone, and the sea had retreated before the power of the great machines. An immense brown expanse of land stretched before us, an almost blank slate upon which history was only just beginning to write. The huge dusty space was broken up, articulated by metal fencing, and large signs forbidding various activities, and the concrete and steel foundations of the first tall buildings; also pile drivers, stream-rollers, trucks, wheel-barrows, cranes.
>
> *(1999: 204)*

Rai believes that the desert-like emptiness of the construction site is symbolic of the "desert of the spirit" (1999: 204); however, his father surmises that this is "the empty canvas," which, with the artists' intervention might bring forth the "Ozymandian colossi" of the mighty from where they can look down upon the city. While Rai's father, despite his late ironic sympathy with the upcoming city, represents the introverted and romanticized preoccupation with place reflecting the nostalgia of a conservationist who seeks to preserve its heritages; Rai's mother, being a builder, is full of entrepreneurial energy responsible for fragmenting, instrumentalizing, and homogenizing of space by the unfeeling capitalist programmes, and thus, eventually erroneously siding with the corrupted Piloo Doodhwala. On the other hand, Rushdie's vision of recovering of place is aestheticized in Rai, the photographer's, different response to the city. He photographs the city at moments of "exists" such as funerals, airports, and cinemas, which, much like Rushdie's depiction, becomes an effective way of preserving the unique city as a process. *The Satanic Verses* does not have any specific reference to the land-reclamation. However, Rashmi Verma rightly points out that the instance of Saladin Chamcha coming back to Bombay finally to find out that his ancestral property is worth millions and is ready to be sold off to the developers by Sala-din's stepmothers unsentimentally effectively illustrates this proposition "One more high-rise, one less piece of old Bom-bay ... What's the difference? Cities change" (535)9. In the 1980s, a bungalow amidst the vertical skyline of Scandal point, a neighbourhood near Marine Drive, would naturally be an immensely coveted property for the real-estate developers. Although in this novel, there is a reconciliation of Saladin with his father and his home city Bombay, yet Saladin's "return" is not unproblematic as the novel is left open-ended, thereby raising questions of the authenticity of Saladin's romanticized homecoming to the lost city of his childhood.

Chronologically, Rushdie's novels depict Bombay through the decades of the 1950s to the early 1990s, a period marked by postcolonial modernity rather than postmodern globalization. The urban development projects, especially in the Backbay area, reflect nation-building ideals. However, Rushdie's novels are replete with unreliable narration of history. In *The Ground Beneath Her Feet*, Bombay in the 1970s "had become Mumbai" under Piloo Doodhwala's MA party (1999: 215); this actually happened in 1995 under the Shiv Sena government. Therefore some of the concerns of the "placelessness" of globality is preponed in Rushdie's landscape of Bombay; and while in many cases Rushdie's sense of place is an anticipation, but in a certain way it is also a documentation of a global sense of place especially as it emerges as an antidote to nativist claims of monolithic identities of place, such as Shiv Sena's renaming of Bombay as Mumbai privileging the Marathi identity of Bombay over its other identities. In *The Moor's Last Sigh*, there are two competing villainous forces—the capitalist Abraham Zogoiby and the communalist Mainduck Fielding, the latter being a thinly veiled caricature of the Shiv Sena supreme Bal Thackeray. But in *The Ground Beneath*

Her Feet, Rushdie coalesces both these villainous forces in the figure of Piloo Doodhwala, recognizing that they are the two sides of the same coin. Zogoiby's capitalist ventures, in readying Bombay with the looks of a global metropolis, result in stripping places of their unique identities. Stemming from the parochial yearnings of the comforts, security, and the material advantages of a monolithic, straightforward place-based identity is the reactionary and the destructive politics of the nativist parties such as the Fielding's Mumbai Axis; Piloo Doodhwala in being a corrupt builder and a neo-conservative politician merges both these forces. Bombay suffered from a grisly communal riot in 1992 after the demolition of Babri Masjid in Ayodhya by Hindu fundamentalist forces and endured subsequent serial blasts seen as retaliation to the riots by the predominantly Muslim underworld. Tangentially alluding to the real-life tragedy, in the wake of the blasts destroying the landscape of the city, Moraes Zogoiby leaves Bombay for Spain in *The Moor's Last Sigh.* In *The Ground Beneath Her Feet,* there is a similar abandonment—Rai in the "decisive moment" of leaving Bombay, following the advice of his photography mentor M. Henri Hulot, identifies the enemy, who not only initiates the near divorce between his parents but also the divorce between Rai and his be-loved Bombay—Piloo Doodhwala. Rai leaves Bombay as the twin forces of urban alienation uniting in "Pilooism won the day" (1999: 247).

Conclusion

Rushdie's portrayal of Bombay reveals a deep concern that the city's transformation into an entrepreneurial metropolis threatens to erode its distinctive charms—its idiosyncratic rhythms, whimsical energy, and enchanted lifestyle. As Bombay begins to position itself as a global (post)metropolis, it becomes increasingly efficient and mechanized, gradually succumbing to the monotony and placelessness that often characterize modern urban life. Yet, as Appadurai insightfully notes, cities of the Global South undergo this transformation in unique ways, shaped by their own colonial histories, political cultures, and economic ecologies:

> these cities also produce the social black holes of the effort to embrace and seduce global capital in their own particular ways, which are tied to varied histories (colonial and otherwise), varied political cultures of citizenship and rule, and varied ecologies of production and finance.
>
> *(2011: na)*

However, Rushdie's vision of Bombay does not end with this lament. Rather, he extends it into a critique of the nativist politics that often emerge in response to globalization. These politics manifest both as reactionary resistance to modernity—as seen in Mainduck Fielding in *The Moor's Last*

Sigh—and as opportunistic alignments with global development agendas, exemplified by characters like Piloo Doodhwala in *The Ground Beneath Her Feet*. The legitimacy of groups such as the fictional Mumbai-Axis (mirroring real-world entities like Shiv Sena) is rooted in the ideology of *bhumiputra*, the "sons of the soil," which supports an exclusionary politics that marginalizes non-Marathis—and increasingly, Muslims—in alignment with the broader Hindutva ideology of the Bharatiya Janata Party. This chapter has argued that Rushdie frames the very *land* of Bombay as a process—mutable, constructed, and commodified—rather than a natural or fixed entity. By doing so, he challenges essentialist claims to land and identity, exposing them as rhetorical tools wielded by vested interests. For Rushdie, the right to the city belongs to its *users*—those who inhabit, traverse, and transform it—rather than those who claim it through lineage or legality. Ultimately, Rushdie's Bombay is attuned to the palimpsestic nature of place—a layered, ever-evolving construct increasingly shaped by the flows of global capital in a world of time-space compression. Yet, while acknowledging the transience of place, he resists the totalizing condition of placelessness. He does not seek to nostalgically preserve an idealized heritage of the city, nor does he surrender to homogenizing narratives. Instead, he envisions a "global sense of place" rooted in adaptation, multiplicity, and resistance—a space where alternative futures remain possible.

Episodes involving land reclamation underscore that space in Rushdie's Bombay is not neutral or static but shaped by socio-spatial practices and contested interests. These include both the lived experiences of the city's inhabitants and the interventions of impersonal forces—particularly the corporatized capital and state-sanctioned development that have increasingly reshaped urban landscapes in the Global South. Such forces, often legitimized through the language of modernity and progress, systematically encroach upon and erase lived spaces. Rushdie's narrative resists this erasure. His sense of place critiques not only the top-down restructuring driven by neoliberal development but also the reactionary, exclusionary visions of groups like Shiv Sena, whose ethnic reimagining of Bombay threatens the city's inherent pluralism. Rushdie portrays both as detrimental—one by erasing diversity through homogenizing modernization, the other by tribalizing it into narrow identitarian frameworks. Ultimately, this chapter positions Rushdie's Bombay within Doreen Massey's (1994) framework of a "global sense of place"—a concept that sees places as relational, dynamic, and defined by their connections rather than isolation. This approach allows for a nuanced understanding of identity and community that resists both essentialism and fragmentation. Through the motif of land reclamation, Rushdie's fiction reveals Bombay not just as a backdrop but as a lived, contested, and profoundly meaningful space in the era of globalization.

5

HOUSES OF MEMORIES

Alternative Global Homes in Salman Rushdie's Novels

Rushdie's representations of home, however, offer a critical counterpoint to these trends. Through the lens of Pierre Nora's (1989) concept of *les lieux de mémoire* (sites of memory), his literary homes may be understood as alternative global homes—places where memory, identity, and affect are actively preserved and reconstituted. This chapter argues that the homes depicted in Rushdie's fiction not only reflect the spirit and tensions of globalization but also function as a corrective to its alienating effects. Rather than being performative or commodified, these homes emerge as lived, embodied, and mnemonic spaces—sites of recovery and resistance that are, crucially, conditionally open to the outsider. In this way, Rushdie reimagines home as a place of layered histories and plural affiliations, grounded in memory yet expansively global in its orientation.

Introduction

> It may be that writers in my position, exiles or emigrants or expatriates, are haunted by some sense of loss, some urge to reclaim, to look back, even at the risk of being mutated into pillars of salt. But if we do look back, we must do so in the knowledge—which gives rise to profound uncertainties—that our physical alienation from India almost inevitably means that we will not be capable of reclaiming precisely the thing that was lost; that we will, in short, create fictions, not actual cities or villages, but invisible ones, imaginary homelands. (*Imaginary Homelands* 1991)

While Samir Dayal (1998) identifies Salman Rushdie as "a novelist of interiority, and more specifically of what one might call interior borders—of the domestic rather than the international (notwithstanding his

DOI: 10.4324/9781003106180-5

cosmopolitanism), the psychological rather than the sociological, and the linguistic rather than the objective," he also emphasizes that Rushdie does not disregard the public sphere or political realities, but rather navigates them through the lens of domestic specificities. Similarly, Sara Upstone, in her reading of *Midnight's Children* (1981), contends that domestic spaces in postcolonial fiction are often battlegrounds where colonial and postcolonial tensions unfold. Building on these insights, this chapter investigates the concepts of home and homelessness in Rushdie's novels. Homes in Rushdie's fiction are not fixed, insulated sites but are instead marked by fluidity and displacement. They reflect the lived experiences of migrants and actively deconstruct binary oppositions such as inside/outside or rooted/displaced. Although Rushdie often valorizes the migrant condition—characterized by rootlessness and liminality—his representations of home remain central. The expatriate condition, which informs both Rushdie's personal biography and his literary themes, shapes his portrayal of domestic space as accessed through memory yet grounded in material experience. The homes in his novels forge vital connections to the surrounding city while retaining their own spatial particularity. This chapter thus argues that homes in Rushdie's work—intimate and permeable, conditionally welcoming to outsiders—serve as egalitarian counter-sites to dominant, patriarchal, and exclusionary conceptions of home. In doing so, they resonate with a transnational adaptation of Pierre Nora's concept of les lieux de mémoire (sites of memory), offering a corrective to the condition of global homelessness by anchoring memory and identity in specific, lived spaces.

What Is Home?

The concept of "home" has been extensively theorized in critical socio-spatial discourse, particularly in relation to its interactions and ruptures with the broader world. Gaston Bachelard's *The Poetics of Space* (1969) is foundational in this field, offering a phenomenological reading of domesticity. For Bachelard, home is a site of reverie that shelters the dreamer and connects the individual to cosmic origins through memories and intimate images. Similarly, Martin Heidegger (1971) considers "dwelling" as an ontological mode that brings together mortals, divinities, the sky, and the earth—rooting human existence in space. However, both thinkers express scepticism towards the effects of modern industrialization on traditional domesticity. Their view of home as an "absolute space," to borrow Henri Lefebvre's (1991) term, risks rendering it ahistorical and immune to dialectical analysis. Lefebvre critiques this romanticization by asserting that such depictions obscure the processes of spatial production and the ideological functions of domesticity. Feminist geographers like Dolores Hayden (1980) extend this critique by exposing the gendered dynamics of domestic space. They argue for the deconstruction of the bourgeois ideal of privacy and the normative role of the woman as content domestic labourer. Meanwhile, postcolonial scholars have challenged the universality of Western experiences of home, particularly in the context of migration. For example, Partha Chatterjee (1989) discusses how nationalist elites in colonial India sequestered "home" as a space of tradition, thereby excluding it from modern political engagement. Edward Said (2000), addressing the intellectual in exile, describes home as "contrapuntal" and provisional, a site perpetually out of reach. Homi Bhabha (1992), through his notion of the "unhomely," explores the liminal space of the postcolonial house as one that blurs boundaries between private/public, familiar/unfamiliar, and aesthetic/political.

What Is a Global Home?

In the globalized world, the crisis of homelessness takes many forms. The refugee crisis since 2015, driven by civil wars in Syria, Eritrea, and Afghanistan, and wars between Ukraine and Russia, Israel and Gaza, has brought renewed attention to the plight of forced migrants. These refugees, many of whom sought asylum in Europe, highlight the material urgency of displacement in contemporary geopolitics. However, even affluent nations such as the United States face growing rates of homelessness driven by housing speculation, mortgage instability, and demographic shifts. Beyond forced migration, voluntary movements of highly skilled labourers—the "global cosmopolitans"—also generate new forms of homelessness. These mobile professionals continue a trajectory begun by early twentieth-century third-world intellectuals, but on a vastly expanded and market-oriented scale. Migration, whether forced or voluntary, brings with it not only spatial but also ontological displacement, generating the need to (re)construct home performatively. In this context, scholars like Bill Ashcroft (2001) emphasize the notion of a deterritorialized diasporic home. Ghassan Hage (2010) distinguishes between house-building and home-building, asserting that the latter involves the affective construction of belonging, intimacy, and aspiration. Nostalgia, rather than being regressive, becomes a vital tool for migrants in creating homely spaces. Alison Blunt (2006) similarly argues that displaced communities increasingly reconstruct home through everyday practices, memories, and rituals—making such homes the norm in a migratory world. On the other end of the spectrum, globalization has given rise to technologically advanced "smart homes" and gated communities that reflect both hyper-consumption and increasing social isolation. These spaces, as Mike Davis (1990) notes in his study of Los Angeles, are fortresses of the elite, disconnected from their local environments and marked by surveillance and exclusion. These smart homes also embody the logic of late capitalism, wherein leisure and work spaces are increasingly merged.

Gilles Deleuze (1987) warns that traditional enclosures like the family are giving way to networks of surveillance and modulation under the "society of control." Within this system, individuals are no longer moulded but modulated—reduced to "individuals" managed through data and consumption. These smart homes exemplify this transformation, producing domestic subjects whose identities are shaped less by place than by their function as nodes within global capitalist flows.

Homes as Sites of Memory in Rushdie's Novels

Pierre Nora's (1989) distinction between memory and history is central to understanding the function of memory in Rushdie's novels. According to Nora, "history" and "memory" are not synonymous: history is a critical, fragmented reconstruction of the past, whereas memory is affective and "magical," persisting through living rituals, habits, and embodied practices. In modern secular times, the prioritization of historiography has led to the erosion of sacred environments of memory, leaving behind remnants that Nora terms *les lieux de mémoire* (sites of memory). These sites emerge through the interplay of material and symbolic forces, remembrance and forgetting, continuity and rupture of traditions, and the tension between outward signification and inward self-referentiality. Crucially, they are not abstract or nostalgic but are spatio-temporal, embedded in the texture of the everyday and intertwined with the present. Nora's expansive project conceptualizes sites of memory within the framework of France's national memory, counterposed to the state-regulated official history. However, his model has faced critique from postcolonial scholars for eliding France's imperial past and from memory theorists in the context of globalization, where the nation-state no longer serves as the primary locus for memory politics (Assmann and Conrad, 2010: 6). More recent approaches—such as Astrid Erll's (2011) "travelling memory," Michael Rothberg's (2009) "multidirectional memory," and Ann Rigney's (2014) "multi-sited memory"—emphasize the transnational circulation of traumatic or erased memories across borders and contexts. Departing from these process-oriented models, this chapter instead draws on Susannah Radstone's (2011) call to reclaim the *locatedness* of memory within globalized flows. This theoretical shift enables a reading of Rushdie's homes as peculiar, grounded sites of memory—fragmented yet affectively charged spaces that retain their specificity despite diasporic dislocation. These homes are further characterized by their *schizophrenic* nature. Fredric Jameson (1991) argues that schizophrenia under late capitalism disrupts the formation of memory, as the subject becomes fragmented, dislodged from temporal continuity, and incapable of producing associative or historical meaning. In contrast, Gilles Deleuze views schizophrenia not as a pathology of late capitalism but as a potential mode of resistance—an anti-memory that contests capitalist striations and generates alternative becomings (1987).

Rushdie's fiction negotiates between these poles. While the memories inscribed in his domestic spaces may be schizophrenic, they neither signify the Jamesonian loss of historicity nor fully align with Deleuze's vision of nomadic apathy. Instead, these memories—like those of Gibreel Farishta in *The Satanic Verses* (1988)—reflect an *excess* of historicity, experienced by the postcolonial migrant who is torn between competing, overlapping histories. These nomadic memories remain *localized*, tethered to specific, often haunted, sites. Thus, while Nora's *lieux de mémoire* provide a useful lens, Rushdie modifies this concept by presenting memory sites as schizophrenic and conditionally open to subaltern and marginalized actors. His homes become *located* expressions of deterritorialized memory, retrieving the politics of embodied remembrance in a world increasingly defined by displacement and abstraction.

This dynamic is dramatized in *The Enchantress of Florence* (2008), where Il Machia—a fictionalized Niccolò Machiavelli—seeks to unlock a "palace of memory" embodied in a woman, Angelique, once the slave of the Janissary Argalia. Angelique has been transformed into a vessel of Argalia's military glories, meant to transmit his conquests in the coded language of childhood. This act of encoding memory into her body replicates the patriarchal logic of constructing mausoleums to inscribe male legends over conquered territories. Il Machia's attempt to recover her sovereign self—as both her liberator and master—fails, resulting in her suicide when confronted with the horror of repressed memories and cumulative violations. She thus becomes, in Il Machia's words, a "brothel" rather than a "palace" of memory. Unlike Angelique, the domestic spaces in Rushdie's novels are not mausoleums of male conquest nor patronizing tributes to an idealized feminine selfhood. Instead, they are open, haunted, and affectively rich homes—"emancipatory brothels" that resist patriarchal and nationalist mythologies. These spaces accommodate fractured, contested, and unauthorized claims to domesticity. They offer refuge to the spectral traces of women and the subaltern, challenging the patrilineal logic of collective memory.

Ironically, Angelique's death occurs within a brothel—The House of Mars—run by the formidable La Fiorentina. Though this space challenges the dominant architecture of sovereignty and domesticity, its subversive potential remains privatized and ultimately circumscribed. It does not survive confrontation with the external world. Similar brothels recur in Rushdie's fiction as irreverent, feminized counter-sites to patriarchal power, most notably *The Curtain* in *The Satanic Verses*. Here, under Baal's direction, the brothel stages a satirical inversion of the sacred city of Jahilia by reenacting the Prophet and his twelve wives, thus exposing the performative dimensions of religion and gender. Rushdie seems to suggest that veiling (*purdah*)—often viewed as a tool of Islamist coercion—may also serve as a means of subversive withdrawal, a tactical refusal of social norms enacted within the secretive, conspiratorial intimacy of the feminine domestic sphere. Yet such resistance remains precarious. These alternative spaces are fragile and easily reabsorbed by dominant systems, their autonomy undermined by their detachment from broader political structures.

Rushdie's engagement with veiling and domesticity echoes earlier representations of cloistered female spaces in South Asian Muslim literature. Attia Hosain's *Sunlight on a Broken Column* (1961) portrays the *zenana* as a space that fosters complex female solidarity even while maintaining a strict division from the male public sphere. Though the material zenana may have disappeared, Hosain shows how its ideological traces persist, inscribed on female bodies. A generation later, Sara Suleri in *Meatless Days* (1989) reappraises this legacy, demonstrating how gendered space continues to exist performatively within the "domestic everyday" of traditional Muslim households (Khan, 2004). In Rushdie's fiction, too, the domestic sphere is a site of tension—between repression and resistance, enclosure and expression, memory and erasure.

Homes as Cities in Rushdie's Novels

Repeating the logic of multi-scalar mnemonic strategies, Salman Rushdie, as an expatriate writer, frequently merges the private and intimate sphere of the domestic with the collective and public space of the city. His representations of home often serve as both repositories of memory and allegories for broader historical and political transitions. In *The Moor's Last Sigh* (1995), the houses designed by the young French architect M. Charles Jeanneret, better known as Le Corbusier, challenge the conventional binary between interiority and exteriority. The intrusion of the garden into the first house and the parchment sliding walls of the Japanese-style second house blur the boundaries between inside and outside. This artificiality of walls—symbolizing the porousness of memory and identity—is emblematic of Rushdie's literary homes, where the microcosm of the domestic reflects and refracts the macrocosmic structures of the nation and the globe. The homes in *Midnight's Children* (1981) similarly echo such liminal transitions: the eccentric ritual of William Methwold handing over his colonial estate to new Indian owners at the precise moment of India's independence allegorizes the uneasy inheritance of colonial urban structures and the fragmentation of memory in the postcolonial city of Bombay. In *The Moor's Last Sigh*, the contrast between Elephanta, the aestheticized house of Art located in Malabar Hill, and the sinister Cashondelivery Tower, Abraham Zogoiby's hideout of crime, further illustrates Rushdie's dual vision of

Bombay—romantic and palimpsestic on the one hand, and corrupted and violent on the other. While Elephanta romanticizes Bombay's cosmopolitan legacy through Aurora's Mooristan paintings, Zogoiby's den, reminiscent of Mogambo's lair in the film *Mr. India* (1987), explores the city's underbelly and its descent into organized crime. These dualities are punctuated by the emergence of figures like Mainduck Fielding—a grotesque caricature of Bal Thackeray—whose parochial communal politics transform Bombay's image from an open metropolis to a fractured space of ethno-religious violence. Rushdie continues this architectural and psychological mapping of fractured homes in *Fury* (2001), where Malik Solanka's anonymous New York sublet functions as a Derridean "supplementary home," both compensating for and reflecting the lack left by the domestic traumas of the past. Solanka's failed attempt at self-annihilation in the anonymity of the global city is constantly interrupted by migrant voices—Jewish, Polish, Punjabi—each carrying histories of displacement and trauma, which mirror and amplify his own guarded past. These spectral encounters fracture the apparent erasure of memory in New York's consumerist culture and emphasize that too many unassimilated memories, rather than none, dislocate the migrant's sense of belonging. Neela Mahendra's home, in contrast, is overburdened with a diasporic nostalgia, her obsession with a never-seen homeland reflected in the excess of interior decoration—a haunting architecture of loss.

This thematic of the haunted and contradictory migrant home reaches a symbolic crescendo in *The Golden House* (2017), which allegorizes the implosion of the American Dream through the story of Nero Golden and his three sons. The Golden House, situated in contemporary New York, is a palatial structure built on reinvention and masquerade—an ideal migrant fantasy of success and anonymity. Yet, it is a house torn between extremes: closeness and openness, tradition and modernity, gender fluidity and patriarchal rigidity. Petya, the agoraphobic genius, embodies a claustrophobic withdrawal into intellectual interiority. Apu, the flamboyant artist, embraces an extroverted sensuality, and D, who grapples with gender identity, resists binary categorization altogether. These internal contradictions ultimately prove unsustainable. The house, much like the America it resides in—a nation increasingly hostile to migrants and difference—cannot bear the weight of its constructed fictions. The fall of the Golden family is symbolic of the disintegration of an inclusive, pluralistic vision of America, the alternative West to England. Yet, in this narrative of collapse, Rushdie allows for the emergence of renewal. The true heir to the Golden legacy is not one of Nero's three sons but the child of René, the narrator, and Vasilisa—a hybrid, outsider figure unburdened by the weight of inherited trauma or traditional identities. In this spectral ruinscape, Rushdie plants a fragile hope: even as old migrant homes collapse under the strain of contradictions and

exclusions, new configurations of belonging and inheritance remain possible—ones that do not repeat the past but reimagine it from the margins.
Through this multi-scalar strategy of locating memory within homes that
operate simultaneously as intimate spaces and allegorical sites of historical,
national, and global tension, Rushdie rewrites the politics of memory. His
houses—whether palatial, brothel-like, violent, or spectral—are mnemonic
architectures that conflate personal and collective histories. They reveal the
disjunctive yet entangled registers of postcolonial, diasporic, and global
memory, situated within spaces of disorientation, contradiction, and potential reinvention.

Alternative Global Homes as Sites of Memory in Rushdie's Novels

Beyond "home" as a singular spatial and emotional unit, Salman Rushdie's
novels are populated by smaller, evocative sites of memory—spaces that are
both self-referential in their spatial specificity and associative in their ties
to the cities they inhabit. Modest and often overlooked domestic spaces—
cellars, rooftops, bedrooms, kitchens, windows, thresholds, and everyday
artefacts—operate as symbolic microcosms of the socio-spatial city outside.
These sites are continually updated to reflect the dislocations and anxie-
ties of the globalized world, particularly around ideas of belonging, owner-
ship, and displacement. They serve as repositories of personal and collective
memory, while also unsettling stable notions of domesticity. In *Midnight's
Children*, for instance, the cellar of Aadam Aziz's house in Agra shelters the
fugitive Nadir Khan after the assassination of Mian Abdullah. It eventually doubles as the bedchamber for his marriage to Mumtaz—though the
marriage remains unconsummated. This transformation of the cellar from
a site of political refuge to a secret marital space recalls Gaston Bachelard's
theorization of the house's vertical polarity, where the attic signifies rational
clarity and the cellar irrational repression. Rushdie's cellar, however, collapses these distinctions, becoming the site of a grotesque familial secret
that re-emerges in the body of Saleem Sinai, marked by impotence. The
unconsummated union becomes a ghostly talisman, reinforcing the family's
openness to outsiders by prefiguring their later acceptance of Saleem, despite
the revelation that he is not their biological child. Artefacts, too, become
charged with mnemonic power. The spittoon—originally a toy in a childhood game played by Nadir Khan—survives the bombing that annihilates
Saleem's family in Pakistan. Like the perforated sheet through which Aadam
Aziz glimpses his future wife in fragments, the spittoon defies normative
domestic boundaries. It carries traces of subversive energies: the irrepress-
ible Rani of Cooch Naheen, the impish elders of Agra, and the revolutionary
Nadir Khan himself. These objects embody resilience beyond blood ties or

heterosexual domesticity, turning into vessels for a more collective, inclusive lineage.

The perforated sheet, in contrast, symbolizes the persistence of tradition. It mediates the origins of the Sinai family line through a fragmented, courtship gaze and later becomes emblematic of a stifling marital routine. Both objects—spittoon and sheet—gesture towards Bombay as a city that is at once inviting and excluding. While Rushdie celebrates its cosmopolitan embrace, the city's impoverished and disenfranchised populations are only fleetingly acknowledged. In *The Moor's Last Sigh*, this erasure contributes to the city's collapse, as sectarian forces such as the Shiv Sena exploit the very cracks that Rushdie's narrative sidesteps. Rushdie also complicates Bachelard's spatial dichotomy between attic and cellar by imbuing rooftops with uncanny energy. In *Midnight's Children*, Mary, the nurse who swaps Saleem with Shiva, sees a ghost on the roof that turns out to be her former communist lover, Joseph D'Costa. His mistaken killing symbolizes the commercial city's paranoia towards its repressed ideological underside—a tension echoed in the real-world repression of Bombay's textile mill strikes led by Dr Datta Samant, dramatized in *The Moor's Last Sigh*.

In *The Satanic Verses*, another arboreal artefact—the walnut tree in the courtyard of Saladin Chamcha's childhood home—emerges as a living site of memory. The tree anchors Saladin's untainted boyhood in Bombay. Its chopping, ordered by his father Changez for commercial gain, signals the severing of Saladin's emotional ties to his past. In its place, memory persists only as a grotesque, mummified presence—such as Ayah Kasturba's transformation into a mirror image of Saladin's dead mother. Yet the magic lamp in the Chamchawala household holds out a different promise: the fantasy of return, of recovering the lost home through enchanted memory. It offers, simultaneously, the possibility of miraculous regression and the realization that such return is illusory in a rational, adult world. Windows and casements in Rushdie's fiction function as thresholds between interior and exterior, memory and history. In *Shame*, the gothic house in Nishapur—home to Omar Khayyam and his three unwed mothers—is a liminal, sovereign space located between cantonment and bazaar. Detached from both colonial modernity and traditional patriarchy, it stages a feminist defiance until Omar gazes out the window at twelve and glimpses Farah Zoroaster, introducing adolescent male desire into the insulated space. This breach reterritorializes shameless feminine autonomy into patriarchal violence in Karachi, transforming a space of resistance into one of oppression.

Windows recur in *The Moor's Last Sigh*, where nursery walls painted with "windows both of and on the world of make-believe" grant young Moraes a repertoire of identities rooted in artifice and disguise. These counterfeit portals furnish him with tools of metamorphosis—strategies essential for survival in a city increasingly hostile to difference. In Shiv Sena–dominated Mumbai, performative identity becomes a form of resistance. Thresholds and their gatekeepers further dramatize the porous boundaries of Rushdie's domestic spaces. In *The Moor's Last Sigh*, Aurora Zogoiby's household at Elephanta employs the sailor Lambajan Chandiwala, an Indianized Long John Silver, as both protector and facilitator of transgression. While Lambajan ostensibly guards Elephanta from the outside world, he also exposes Moraes to the city's unruly underbelly—from crowded trams and street food to clandestine escapades. His wife, Jaya He, similarly functions as a mediator between the elite and the popular city. Rather than maintain boundaries, these figures enable a flow between privileged and marginal spaces, reflecting Rushdie's broader ambivalence about the inclusivity of Bombay.

Such ambivalence pervades Rushdie's depiction of characters who occupy in-between spaces. Saleem, biologically an outsider, is accepted into the Sinai family. In *Shame*, Omar Khayyam—socially and genealogically ambiguous—is absorbed into the elite of Karachi. In *The Satanic Verses*, the goatman Saladin Chamcha finds shelter with illegal migrants in Shandaar Café. In *The Enchantress of Florence*, Niccolò Vespucci is welcomed by Emperor Akbar not through lineage but through storytelling. These narratives portray cities as sites of conditional hospitality, where inclusion hinges on performance and approval by dominant heteropatriarchal norms. Bedrooms, finally, are the most intimate and volatile of Rushdie's mnemonic spaces. They host scenes of incest, illegitimacy, secrecy, and desire, often conflicting with the patriarchal imperative to institutionalize lineage. Saleem's awkward sexual encounters in *Midnight's Children*, his romantic longing for his sister Jamila, Salahuddin's masturbation in *The Satanic Verses*, and the alleged sexual violation of Moraes by his mother and sisters in *The Moor's Last Sigh* all point to the bedroom as a contested terrain. It harbours both liberation and repression, queer desire and normative constraint. It is the site of lesbian intimacy in *Shame*, extramarital affairs in *The Satanic Verses* and *The Moor's Last Sigh*, and mystic-ritualistic unions in *The Enchantress of Florence*. Bedrooms, in Rushdie, become gateways not only to the sociospatial realities of the city but also to myth, dream, and the supernatural. Gibreel Farishta's transformation into the archangel Gibreel in his sleep, for instance, dramatizes this transition from domestic interiority to cosmic enactment.

In Rushdie's novels, domestic spaces are rarely insulated. Instead, they function as volatile intersections between memory, identity, and urban geography. Cellars, rooftops, windows, and bedrooms are not static backdrops but animated, haunted, and often enchanted sites of personal and political significance. They reflect the porous boundaries of Rushdie's fictional homes and the cities they inhabit—ever shifting, inclusive yet exclusionary, rooted yet dislocated. A persistent tension animates Rushdie's fiction between free, illegitimate, subversive notions of home and city, and the structures of institutionalized patriarchy—nowhere more strikingly than in *Shame*, which foregrounds the repression of feminine sexuality. In Raza Hyder's household, the communal bedchamber—where wives are consigned with spinster cousins as their husbands work in distant cities—epitomizes this dynamic. This spatial arrangement, ostensibly designed to safeguard chastity under the surveillance of an elderly matriarch, paradoxically enables transgression: in the darkness, husbands stealthily seek out their wives, leading to mistaken identities and acts of infidelity. Such moments expose the fraught interplay between the repressed sexual codes of the hinterlands and the more openly expressed sexualities of metropolitan spaces.

The patriarchal fantasy of a virginal bedchamber—where female sexuality is tightly policed—finds a counterpart in another utopia: a resplendent conjugal space dedicated to producing multiple male heirs, affirming familial continuity and patriarchal virility. Yet this ideal frequently collapses under its own weight. Naveed Hyder, for instance, commits suicide after bearing several children, unable to withstand the pressures of continued reproduction for her military husband. Her sister, the mentally retarded Sufiya Zinobia, remains a virgin in marriage to Omar Khayyam, whose desires are instead satisfied by her ayah. In these homes, female sexuality is channelled solely towards the gratification of male desire—desire that is inseparably linked to territorial and socio-spatial control. Across Rushdie's novels, acts of transgressive female sexuality are met with violent patriarchal retribution. In *Midnight's Children*, the destruction of Saleem's family in a bombing coincides with his incestuous love for his sister. In *The Moor's Last Sigh*, the adulterous liaisons of Aurora Zogoiby unravel her marriage to Abraham and catalyze the fall of their estate, Elephanta, perched on Malabar Hill. In *The Satanic Verses*, Pamela, pregnant with Jumpy Joshi's illegitimate child, dies with him in a fire at the Shandaar Café. Meanwhile, *Shame* offers its most violent counterpoint: the monstrous, rage-filled figure of Sufiya Zinobia. Rather than create domestic order or creative continuity—associated with an Apollonian ideal of home—she embodies Dionysian destruction, her suppressed desire erupting in spectral violence.

Rushdie's bedrooms often become the stage for such confrontations, staging open conflicts between female rage and male transgression. In *Fury*, the bedroom of Malik Solanka becomes a site of seriocomic drama, where wife, ex-lover, and girlfriend confront his infidelities. This explosive altercation produces a moment of catharsis, liberating both men and women from the claustrophobia of repressed desire. Across these texts, Rushdie suggests that a sustainable model of home lies not in repression or unchecked transgression but in a negotiated balance between subversive, fluid sexualities and the structures of familial normativity. The feminine domestic space of the kitchen emerges as another critical site of memory, conflict, and cultural hybridity. In *The Moor's Last Sigh*, the kitchen functions as a microcosm of Bombay's multiculturalism—blending Anglo-Indian, South Indian, Mughlai, Kashmiri, Goan, Hyderabadi, and Bombay club cuisines (Rushdie, 1995: 296). This gastronomic syncretism reflects a different ethos from the city's social and economic exclusions, where food becomes a medium of mingling and resistance. The impurity and hybridity of food in Rushdie's fiction stand in ironic contrast to the politics of purity espoused by intolerant, fundamentalist figures. Even the kitchen of Mainduck Fielding, a parochial politician who reviles cultural mixtures, is infiltrated by this unruly hybridity. Yet, despite its subversive potential, the politics of food remains limited in scope—it does not radically transform the city's dominant power structures.

Kitchens are not unambiguously liberatory in Rushdie's work. They are often spaces of intrigue and revelation. In *The Moor's Last Sigh*, the cook Ezekiel's diary reveals to Moraes the infidelity that haunts his parents' marriage, casting doubts over his legitimacy. In *Midnight's Children*, the kitchen becomes a battleground of ideological and domestic conflict when Reverend Mother barricades it in protest of Aadam Aziz's expulsion of the Maulvi, who had been preaching religious intolerance. In response, Aziz begins a hunger strike. This symbolic act—a Muslim doctor rejecting food to defend secular education—parodies the Gandhian satyagraha and critiques both religious orthodoxy and nationalist myth-making. Aziz's resistance prefigures broader patterns in Rushdie's fiction, where small acts of domestic dissent echo in the larger political and global sphere. Indeed, Rushdie frames religious fundamentalism and terrorism not only as geopolitical phenomena but also as extensions of failed domesticity. In *Shalimar the Clown*, Islamic terrorism is portrayed as a magnified drama of broken homes and unresolved domestic violence. Dr Aziz's quiet defiance against the mock tyranny of his wife in *Midnight's Children* becomes, retrospectively, a lesson in resilience—echoed in the global context of post-*Satanic Verses* threats, including the fatwa from Ayatollah Khomeini.

Even in *Fury*, domestic interiors—particularly kitchens—become crucibles of suppressed emotion and potential violence. Malik Solanka's murderous rage crescendos in the solitude of his kitchen, where he contemplates killing his sleeping wife and child with a kitchen knife. This moment of psychological crisis may be read as a return of repressed trauma from his Bombay childhood, where he was abused by his stepfather. His flight from London to New York transforms this private rage into a symptom of a broader diasporic condition: the fury of displaced migrants who carry fractured homes across cities, haunted by what they flee and yet doomed to re-enact it. Across Rushdie's novels, kitchens, bedrooms, rooftops, and bed-chambers become intimate arenas where global politics, historical trauma, and ideological battles are staged. These spaces do not merely reflect the cities they inhabit; they anticipate them, foreshadow their fractures, and embody their possibilities. Whether as sites of transgression, subversion, negotiation, or memory, the domestic interiors in Rushdie's work are never enclosed—they are permeable, unstable, and deeply political.

Conclusion

This chapter has examined the multifaceted portrayals of home in Salman Rushdie's novels as imaginative, alternative global homes—fluid, ambivalent, and deeply embedded in memory. These homes are not static sanctuaries but modified, often schizophrenic spaces, bearing the weight of personal histories, cultural dislocation, and socio-political turbulence. They embody a paradox: on the one hand, they are conditionally accommodating and inclusive, offering fractured yet meaningful forms of belonging; on the other, they reveal the deep tensions of exclusion, surveillance, and displacement that characterize life in the global city. Rushdie's fictional homes resonate with Saskia Sassen's notion of global cities as "frontier zones" of both hyper-connectivity and conflict (Sassen, 2012). These urban spaces, while celebrated for their cosmopolitan openness, frequently welcome only the economically desirable—primarily skilled migrants—through selective hospitality governed by neoliberal capitalism. For the rest, especially the displaced, the refugee, or the culturally unassimilable, the city becomes increasingly "unhomely," a site of perpetual precarity and rejection. In this context, Rushdie's domestic interiorse merge as counter-narratives to the exclusionary logic of the global city, offering intimate, defiant articulations of belonging that resist commodification and erasure.

The homes in Rushdie's novels challenge dominant categories of legitimate insider and illegitimate outsider. They refuse to conform to the binaries of host and guest, citizen and migrant, centre and periphery. Instead, they stage moments of hybridity, negotiation, and resistance that anticipate and respond to the contemporary global crisis of homelessness—not only in the literal sense of physical dislocation but also as a profound psychic and cultural unmooring. In Rushdie's fictional universe, home is neither a fixed geography nor a nostalgic ideal; it is a site of becoming, shaped through memory, language, trauma, and desire. Crucially, the domestic spaces in Rushdie's fiction are not performative stages of migrant nostalgia, nor are they sanitized products of global consumerist fantasy. Unlike the polished homes of global elites—curated, commodified, and stripped of memory—Rushdie's homes are textured, lived-in, and emotionally charged. They pulsate with contradictions, serving as both sanctuaries and battlegrounds, sites of oppression and resistance, continuity and rupture. Through these richly imagined domestic spheres, Rushdie reimagines the very idea of global home—one that is not rooted in stability or purity, but in multiplicity, memory, and the ongoing negotiation of identity in an unsettled world.

6

THE PRODUCTION OF ALTERNATIVE GLOBAL SPACES

Walking in the City in Salman Rushdie's Novels

Introduction

> I walked the city like a ghost, through streets whose names I had known but whose faces were changed. My feet carried me past memories ... with every step I took, I was walking through the ruins of my past, and the wreckage of a city that had once been mine. (*The Moor's Last Sigh* 1995)

Michel de Certeau's seminal essay "Walking in the City" (1984: 91–110) conceptualizes walking as a subversive and resistant practice. This notion has since been revisited in contemporary theories of affect and posthumanism, which advocate a renewed focus on the body and the human, albeit in more fluid and decentred terms. These newer frameworks propose a reconfigured walker who blurs traditional binaries such as subject/object and human/non-human, thereby advancing a contested embodiment and an inclusive mode of self-fashioning that accommodates alterity. Salman Rushdie, too, mobilizes the motif of walking in the city as a transformed act of resistance. In his novels, walking becomes a practice that dismantles the autonomy of the walker's body upon its encounter with the material cityscape, aligning with post-anthropocentric discourses. However, this fragmentation of bodily autonomy is shaped by a transformed body politic, particularly resonant for migrant figures from the global South, as opposed to the more localized, rooted walkers of the Global North.

This chapter argues that walking in Rushdie's urban landscapes generates alternative global spatialities. To examine these emergent global spaces, the chapter investigates the walkers' bodies as sites of multi-scalar embodied memory—memory that extends beyond the corporeal into the tactile and material fabric of the city. Building upon the mnemonic potential of

DOI: 10.4324/9781003106180-6

embodied movement, the analysis traces how walkers conjure spectral remnants of the past, rendering the city a haunted, affective topography marked by sensual and corporeal interactions. Furthermore, the chapter interrogates the heterogeneous gazes of walkers in Rushdie's fiction, which oscillate between elitist detachment and participatory immersion, thereby reworking de Certeau's image of the confident, metropolitan, anthropocentric flâneur. Some of Rushdie's walkers are even figured as posthuman, monstrous entities—simultaneously marginal and resistant to mechanisms of biopolitical control and identity regulation. Finally, the chapter explores how Rushdie's walkers spatialize the city vertically through his imaginative invocation of a tripartite universe—comprising the subterranean, the terrestrial, and the celestial. This vertical orientation disrupts the flat, instantaneous cartographies characteristic of global modernity, offering instead a layered, temporally charged alternative to contemporary urban spatiality.

Walking in the City: From Walter Benjamin to Posthuman Walkers

The trope of walking in the city has long served as a critical lens for exploring public space, particularly in theories of spatiality that foreground the body politic of the walker in relation to the increasingly alienating landscapes of modern and postmodern urban environments. Walter Benjamin's reading of the flâneur, especially in his engagement with Baudelaire's heroic artist (1997: 35–66), positions this figure as both a product and a casualty of the modern city. The abandonment of the Parisian arcades signals a melancholic rupture—marking the loss of the flâneur's nostalgic, contemplative gaze in the face of the burgeoning commodification of everyday life in the emerging consumer metropolis.

With Michel de Certeau, however, the focus shifts from the passive observer to the active participant. In his influential essay "Walking in the City," walking becomes an act of spatial enunciation—generating a "mobile" city composed of personal memories, stories, superstitions, and myths. For de Certeau, the pedestrian intervenes in the homogenized, corporatized, and abstract urban grid, transforming it through embodied practices rooted in the everyday. The walker's resistance emerges not from a position of authorial mastery but from a vulnerable, lived engagement with space. This body politic of the pedestrian parallels Henri Lefebvre's theory of "rhythmanalysis" (*Rhythmanalysis*), which emphasizes the body's polyrhythmic interaction with the regimented tempos of technocratic rationality within the urban environment. However, both Lefebvre and de Certeau stop short of conceptualizing the fragmented, posthuman body of the twenty-first-century walker navigating the deterritorialized, digitally networked city.

Nigel Thrift (2004) critiques de Certeau's anthropocentric bias, offering an alternative perspective that shifts from walking to driving as a mode of spatial engagement. For Thrift, the automobile becomes an extension of the human body—part of a "technological unconscious"—that codes the city not through traditional binaries of author/reader or consumer/spectator but through participatory and algorithmic interfaces. This shift gestures towards a more radical reconceptualization of embodiment, drawing from Gilles Deleuze's notion of the *machinic body* (1987), Bruno Latour's *actor-network theory* (2005), Donna Haraway's *cyborg feminism* (1985), and species theory (2007), all of which emphasize the body's permeability, virtuality, and entanglement with non-human actors. In these frameworks, the body is no longer a self-contained, stable entity but a *material-semiotic* construct that exceeds the boundaries of skin and identity. Such a body deconstructs the binaries of self/other, human/non-human, and nature/technology. Rosi Braidotti (2013) identifies this as the *posthuman condition*—a state in which the historical "others" of the Renaissance ideal (as exemplified by Da Vinci's Vitruvian Man)—namely women, colonized peoples, and animals— are no longer excluded from the category of the human but are integral to its very constitution. Rather than emphasizing techno-utopian transcendence, Braidotti proposes an affirmative posthuman politics grounded in hybridity and informed by Edward Said's critique of Orientalism, wherein the "other" is repositioned not in opposition to but within the space of the human.

The figure of the walker, traditionally visualized as the solitary male subject adrift in a disenchanted urban space, has also been critically interrogated through feminist and postcolonial lenses. The conspicuous absence of the *flâneuse*—the female walker—in canonical accounts of modernity has been highlighted by scholars such as Janet Wolff (1985) and Griselda Pollock (1988), who point to the gendered exclusions embedded in public space. Doreen Massey (1994) adds a global dimension through her concept of the *power geometry* of time-space compression, which reveals how mobility is unevenly distributed along axes of gender, race, and class. In the cities of the Global South, these disparities are further exacerbated: for many women, the urban street remains a precarious and often violent space, necessitating collective movement, male chaperones, or restricted access. Given this context, the act of walking in postcolonial cities becomes an important site of contestation. Scholars such as Anjali Gera Roy (2007) illustrate how walking in spaces like Lucknow's *Chowk* reveals suppressed narratives— such as those of Punjabi refugee colonies—that are effaced in dominant representations of the Nawabi city. Similarly, Rashmi Varma (2012), Claire Chambers (2014), and Sara Upstone (2009) have examined the differential politics of walking in postcolonial urban contexts, emphasizing how spatial practices intersect with class, caste, gender, and migration.

Thus, in the contemporary global city, walking is no longer an act confined to a bounded, male, autonomous subject. Instead, it engenders a fluid affective state in which the body is constantly fractured, mediated, and reconstituted through intersecting discourses of gender, race, class, post-coloniality, and technology. The walker becomes a contested, mutable, and autopoietic figure—a subject in motion who embodies and negotiates multiple vulnerabilities and agencies. In the sections that follow, this chapter mobilizes these theoretical perspectives to analyze how Rushdie's novels both engage with and subvert dominant models of walking. Positioned as a writer of the Global South, Rushdie reimagines the act of walking through characters whose trajectories disrupt stable notions of urban space, identity, and embodiment, offering a distinctive intervention into the literature of spatial mobility and resistance.

Walkers as Multi-Scalar Embodied Memory

Salman Rushdie's novels often trace journeys into the past, engaging with memories of lost homes in India and Pakistan. These texts function as novels of memory, where walking in the city emerges as a key narrative and thematic act of embodied remembrance. In Rushdie's urban landscapes, walking does not merely signify physical movement—it becomes a mnemonic practice, echoing the recursive narrative structures of his fiction. Paul Connerton (1989: 72–104) conceptualizes the body as a repository of embodied memory, carrying both voluntary and involuntary recollections within its gestures and rhythms. In Rushdie's novels, however, the walkers' bodies operate as *multi-scalar* sites of memory—at once personal, historical, and geopolitical. These bodies form mnemonic assemblages with the cities they traverse, mapping intimate recollections onto urban materiality. In *Fury* (2001), Malik Solanka's erratic and disoriented walks through New York suggest a deliberate erasure of memory. Haunted by the traumas of an abused childhood in Bombay and a failed marriage in London, Solanka performs a kind of urban amnesia. Yet paradoxically, the very fury he suppresses disseminates across the city, animating other figures like Majnu, the brash, disillusioned migrant taxi driver, and even the affluent American serial killers. Through these spectral projections, Solanka's internal turmoil becomes externalized, refracted through the bodies and actions of other urban characters. His disembodied rage circulates, inflecting the psychic and moral landscape of New York.

In *Shalimar the Clown* (2005), the body itself becomes a site of visualized memory. When India, the daughter of a diplomat, first encounters Shalimar, her father's new driver, she sees his body bloom into the landscape of Kashmir: "His hair was a mountain stream. There were narcissi from the banks of rushing rivers and peonies from the high meadows growing from his chest, poking out through his open collar. Around him raucously echoed the sound of swarnai" (11). Shalimar's body, in this moment, is not merely a metaphor for the Shalimar Bagh—it becomes a literal embodiment of the Kashmiri landscape and its lost idyll. India, in turn, mirrors the memory of his lost love Boonyi, her mother, thus becoming a living palimpsest of the violence and longing tied to Kashmir. Both characters extend the trauma and beauty of Kashmir into the urban present of Los Angeles, thereby mapping a geopolitical memory onto the city's everyday spaces. In this transposition, cities such as Los Angeles and Kashmir are woven into a global network of embodied memory and political violence. Across Rushdie's fiction, embodied memory frequently materializes in spectral form, externalized through phantoms from actual or imagined pasts. In *Midnight's Children* (1981), Saleem Sinai's urban wanderings in Bombay and Karachi retrace the fragmented journeys of his counterfeit lineage, reanimating ancestral figures through new avatars. His grandfather Aadam Aziz's journey from Kashmir to Punjab and Agra traces India's colonial past through a series of episodic, picaresque encounters. A generation later, Saleem's father, Ahmed Sinai, migrates from colonial Delhi to postcolonial Bombay and Karachi, navigating a series of failed entrepreneurial ventures that echo the disillusionment of the newly independent nation. Saleem's own ambulations through these cities refract these layered histories. In Bombay, his act of secretly following his mother to the Pioneer Café connects him to Nadir Khan—linking Bombay's subterranean world of struggling artists and leftist activists with the earlier story of Nadir hiding in a cellar in Agra, sheltered by Aadam Aziz and briefly married to Saleem's mother. This spatial overlap constructs a mnemonic bridge across cities and generations, fusing personal memory with national history.

Similarly, in Karachi, Saleem's extraordinary olfactory powers guide him to Tai Bibi, a mythical, transgressive figure whose decaying body recalls the ancient boatman Tai of Kashmir. Both characters, olfactorily marked and politically unruly, resist the rationalizing forces of colonial and postcolonial authority. Tai Bibi's spectral presence in the rigid, masculinist space of Karachi resonates with Tai's presence in colonial Kashmir, symbolizing an enduring, embodied challenge to systemic power. Moreover, the recurrence of mob violence across Saleem's narrative arc reveals another form of embodied memory—one rooted in collective trauma. The language riots in Bombay, where Dr Narlikar is killed, mirror the earlier communal riots in pre-independence Delhi, in which Lifafa Das is nearly lynched by a frenzied crowd but is saved by Saleem's mother. These moments of urban violence, geographically and temporally dispersed, converge through Saleem's narrative and physical movement, emphasizing how the city absorbs, stores, and replays memory through bodies and space. In all these instances, walking functions as a deeply affective practice through which the city becomes an archive of multi-scalar memory—where the individual body, family history, national trauma, and global conflict intersect. Rushdie's walkers do not merely traverse space; they *produce* it as memory, as affect, as politics.

The Walks in Rushdie's Novels Expose an Affective City

In Rushdie's novels, walking in the city not only mobilizes memory—it generates affective urban landscapes saturated with sensory intensity and spectral presence. The notion of the spectre expands here into the idea of the affective city: a space shaped by the body's entanglement with the rhythms, resistances, and invitations of urban life. Gregory J. Seigworth and Melissa Gregg define affect as "persistent proof of a body's never less than ongoing immersion in and among the world's obstinacies and rhythms, its refusals as much as its invitations" (2010: 1). Affect, in this context, emerges as the residue and resonance of bodily encounters with the world—non-linear, non-representational, and deeply immersive. Henri Lefebvre's *Rhythmanalysis* (1992/2004) offers a complementary framework, emphasizing the rhythmic belonging—or non-belonging—of the body to the temporality of the city. For Lefebvre, the modern urban subject, increasingly shaped by visual saturation under (post)capitalism, must relearn to *hear* the city. Vision, he warns, is the most manipulated and abused sense in urban modernity; the true rhythmanalyst attunes instead to auditory and affective frequencies.

Rushdie's cities, particularly Bombay, are often constructed through the acoustics of urban life. The rhythms of the city are encoded in speech, dialect, and dissonance. This is most vividly performed in *The Moor's Last Sigh* (1995), where the voice of Aurora Zogoiby bursts forth in exaggerated, polyphonic Bombay English—her speech becoming an affective soundscape that evokes a hyper-real version of the city. Similarly, Rushdie employs olfactory imagination to evoke spatial complexity. Saleem Sinai's heightened sense of smell in *Midnight's Children* maps a blurred topography of Karachi, one that resists binary categorization. Smell here functions like affect: intangible, destabilizing, and boundary-dissolving. It undermines distinctions between subject and object, sacred and profane, self and city.

Although Rushdie is not typically known for detailed spatial description, his novels foreground the sensory and affective experience of space. The body, always partially alienated, becomes a key site of urban encounter. In *Midnight's Children*, Amina Sinai's walk through the narrow alleys of Old Delhi erodes her "city eyes"—a perceptual unlearning that exposes the subaltern and marginalized city beyond the sanitized colonial modernity of Lutyens's Delhi. Her discomfort intensifies as she sees maimed beggars, impoverished children, and a grotesque British drag queen—an allegorical figure for the crumbling imperial order. Her passage through this "infernal city," particularly while accompanied by Lifafa Das, places her in a state of embodied anxiety. Similarly, Aurora Zogoiby in *The Moor's Last Sigh* performs the role of artist-walker as she navigates the chaotic streets of Bombay in search of subjects for her hyperreal "Chipkali" paintings. Her urban wandering is not simply voyeuristic; it leads to acts of transgression and accident. While covering the landlubber strike, Aurora runs over a naval officer, later employing him as a gatekeeper. This moment of guilt and gendered vulnerability disrupts her usual posture of nonchalance. Both Amina and Aurora, though elite by class, experience a gendered precarity in the marginal zones of the city—an affective (non)belonging that complicates their roles as detached observers. Their bodily discomforts, as women moving through masculinized and marginalized urban space, create zones of anxiety where the subject-spectator and the objectified spectacle collapse into one another.

Art itself becomes a portal of affective engagement in Rushdie's cityscapes. Simon O'Sullivan describes art as "a portal, an access point, to another world (our world experienced differently), a world of impermanence and interpenetration, a molecular world of becoming" (2001: 128). His notion of "transhuman aesthetics" underscores the power of art to fracture self-preservation, to exceed anthropocentric perspectives, and to access a sensuous, non-human mode of worlding. This is exemplified in *The Ground Beneath Her Feet*, where Rai, the photographer-walker, documents the city through his "photography of exits." Rather than capturing the everyday life of Bombay, Rai focuses on transit zones—airports, cinemas, funeral processions—liminal sites where one world bleeds into another. His art, shaped by absence, is resistant precisely because it reveals the limitations of the subjective eye. By emphasizing the threshold rather than the dwelling, Rai produces an affective city in flux—one that resists stabilization or containment.

Rushdie further complicates the notion of the walking subject through instances of *proxy-walking*, where characters access the city through the sensory perceptions of others. In *Midnight's Children*, Saleem follows his mother to the Pioneer Café not by foot but through telepathic extension. He accesses the sordid zones of Bombay through Amina's vision, blurring the lines between observer and observed. Similarly, in *The Enchantress of Florence* (2008), Emperor Akbar walks the streets of Florence not physically but through the stories of Niccolò Vespucci. This imaginative traversal reverses the gaze of Orientalism, as the Mughal emperor exoticizes the West. In both cases, the affective experience of the city is mediated through another's body or narrative, producing a sensuous city that is not a transparent landscape but a textured, unstable field of perception. Ultimately, Rushdie's urban walkers—whether actual, imagined, or proxy—do not merely move through space. Their walks *generate* affective cities: sensorial, unstable, and alive with rhythms, smells, and spectral echoes. These cities are not clearly mapped geographies but are constituted through the porous, anxious, and affectively charged movements of bodies in flux.

The Disrupted Gaze: Walking and Driving in Rushdie's Cities

Michel de Certeau's seminal essay "Walking in the City" (1984) opens with a commanding view from the now-demolished World Trade Center, where the panoramic gaze allows for a distanced, totalizing vision of the city. This ocular privilege, however, transforms the viewer into a voyeur— removed from the grasp of the city's rhythms, people, and unpredictability. De Certeau contrasts this elevated, imperial gaze with the tactile, grounded practices of everyday walkers, who inventively navigate urban life from within its streets. In Salman Rushdie's novels, the act of walking frequently engages with this duality, exposing the complexities of affective belonging, voyeurism, resistance, and the limits of representation in both colonial and postcolonial urban contexts. Rai, the photographer in *The Ground Beneath Her Feet*, personifies the tension between these modes of seeing. Though he attempts to resist the colonial, aerial gaze of photographers like Raja Deen Dayal and A.R. Haseler—whose majestic, elevated views of Bombay reflect imperial control—Rai still struggles to fully inhabit de Certeau's intimate, mobile city. His realist aesthetic, initially trained on grassroots Bombay, eventually turns towards the ephemeral and the transitional—the "photography of exits"—marking funeral processions, airports, and cinemas as fleeting urban nodes of becoming. These spaces, neither fully interior nor exterior, resist representational mastery and evoke what Simon O'Sullivan calls the "transhuman aesthetics" of art—a non-anthropocentric, affective worlding that resists the impulse of self-preservation and control.

Yet, not all walkers in Rushdie's urban spaces succeed in transcending the flâneur's objectifying gaze. Moor Zogoiby's outings in *The Moor's Last Sigh*, or Saladin Chamcha's urban explorations in *The Satanic Verses*, flirt with exoticization, revealing the tension between elite subjectivity and the subaltern spaces they traverse. These walks often reflect the spectacularization of poverty in the cities of the global South, even as Rushdie foregrounds the hesitancy, precarity, and anxiety that mark these encounters. Amina Sinai's walk through Old Delhi in *Midnight's Children* similarly evokes this precarious gaze: her "city eyes" falter amid the labyrinthine alleys, mutilated beggars, and the surreal presence of a ruined drag queen allegorizing the departing Empire. Her walk, pregnant and vulnerable, signals both privilege and fragility, positioning her in a liminal space of affective non-belonging. The disruption of walking is further amplified in moments where the city itself exerts a tactical, even violent resistance to the walker. Aadam Aziz's fall in *Midnight's Children*—while sneezing during the Jallianwala Bagh massacre—underscores the hazardous, tentative nature of walking in the congested, chaotic urban topography of Amritsar. Unlike the Parisian or New York walker celebrated by de Certeau, Rushdie's walkers navigate cities where walking is shaped by class disparity, colonial residue, and infrastructural collapse.

Gibreel Farishta's spatial dyslexia in *The Satanic Verses*, as he wanders the haunted streets of London, reinforces the psychic dislocation of the migrant subject whose right to the city must be forged amid hostility and alienation. Omar Khayyam's vertigo in *Shame* similarly marks walking as a destabilized, vertiginous act. Even the ground itself becomes unreliable in *The Ground Beneath Her Feet*, where devastating earthquakes disorient any notion of stable orientation—an apt metaphor for the diasporic condition. As Olga Volga puts it in *Shalimar the Clown*, everyday life occurs "between the memories and the daily stuff," where movement—like memory—is fragmented, haunted, and constantly negotiated. In *Quichotte* (2019), Rushdie expands his spatial imagination by shifting from walking to driving as the central trope of urban engagement. This narrative shift resonates with Nigel Thrift's critique of de Certeau's privileging of walking in his essay "Driving in the City." Thrift contends that in the posthuman, technologically mediated era, driving offers an equally affective and non-representational interaction with the urban world. The car becomes not merely a vehicle but a site of automation, memory, and mediation.

Ismail Smile, the pharmaceutical salesman protagonist of *Quichotte*, drives across a surreal America with his imagined son Sancho—born from a wish upon a shooting star. The automobile, in this narrative, is both womb and vessel, a "birthing seat" where human and non-human forces converge in acts of creation. Sancho himself is a product of this affective fusion of technoscience, longing, and imagination, symbolizing how postcolonial subjects must invent alternative kinship, memory, and futurity while navigating the fractured terrain of a xenophobic, opioid-ravaged America. Driving, for Ismail Smile, becomes a way of threading through disjointed media landscapes, violent political rhetoric, and the loneliness of diaspora. In contrast to de Certeau's tactile city walkers, Ismail's movement reflects Thrift's "automobility"—a form of engagement less rooted in the physical navigation of space and more in affective mediation through speed, surface, and simulation. The car, in this context, becomes a mobile heterotopia where affective ruptures emerge, allowing moments of introspection, imagination, and resistance within a media-saturated, surveillance-heavy world.

Rushdie's use of driving in *Quichotte* thus builds upon his longstanding interest in destabilized, uncanny urban experience. Here, the city is not something merely to be walked through but something driven into—a blurred terrain where fact and fiction bleed, where the postcolonial subject moves not in mastery but in haunted pursuit. As with the hesitant walkers in his earlier novels, Ismail's drive is marked by anxiety, longing, and the impossible search for connection, offering a nuanced response to both de Certeau and Thrift.

Ultimately, whether through the disruptive, precarious steps of Amina and Aadam or the surreal drives of Ismail and Sancho, Rushdie's fiction foregrounds movement as an affective practice shaped by power, memory, and technology. His cities—Bombay, London, New York—are not fixed cartographies but volatile topographies shaped by migration, myth, and media. In Rushdie's hands, walking and driving are not just acts of movement; they are modalities of becoming, through which his characters navigate the haunted edges of belonging in a globalized world.

Posthuman Monsters as Urban Walkers

In Rushdie's novels, the act of walking—often theorized as an everyday subversive practice in cities of the global North—is reimagined through the disruptive presence of posthuman, monstrous figures who occupy public space. These figures challenge dominant spatial and discursive regimes not through assimilation into normative categories of urban life but by radically deforming them. Rushdie's version of posthumanism does not align with technophilic visions of cybernetic futures; instead, it echoes Rosi Braidotti's (2013) conception of the posthuman as an affirmative politics of inclusion—one that embraces the marginal and monstrous as central to a redefinition of the metropolitan humanist self. This vision extends Edward Said's project of deconstructing colonial binaries, positioning posthuman figures as the next phase in the evolution of decolonial resistance. Rushdie's monsters walk the city as literal embodiments of posthuman hybridity. They are not simply metaphors for alterity; they are corporeal mutations that disturb humanist boundaries. The monster, as a category drawn from both Eastern and Western fables, is traditionally the abjected other of the human. In the postcolonial gothic mode that informs Rushdie's work, these monsters are simultaneously desired and disavowed—figures of anxiety and allure. Jeffrey Jerome Cohen's "Monster Culture (Seven Theses)" (1996/2007) underscores this duality: monsters are hybrid, transgressive, and resist categorization; they inhabit the thresholds of knowledge, identity, and social order.

Rushdie's posthuman monsters take Cohen's formulation further. Rather than remaining hidden or repressed, they emerge as visible, affective agents in the city—what Donna Haraway (1985, 1992) might describe as "inappropriate/d others": cyborgian hybrids that refuse containment. In novels like *The Satanic Verses* and *Shame*, Rushdie uses and parodies religious and mythical motifs to craft a monstrous repertoire rooted in urban political reality. Figures such as the transformed Saladin Chamcha and the feral Sufiya Zinobia, while drawing on the Islamic dastan tradition (e.g., the *adam khor hasina*), are deterritorialized and reassembled to critique the violence of postcolonial societies. Rushdie's monsters operate in two registers. First, there are those who are hidden and confined—Saladin Chamcha's metamorphosis from a successful, deracialized dubbing artist into a satanic goat-man reflects Lucretius's model of metamorphosis: a total rupture from one state to another. This binary model aligns Saladin with the traditional monster, defined in opposition to the normative human and subjected to societal repression. Confined in the Shandaar Café by the sympathetic Abu Simbel, Saladin becomes a symptom of the metropolis's failure to accommodate its own others.

In contrast, Sufiya Zinobia enacts a more fluid, Ovidian metamorphosis—her transformation overlaps with her former self. Already dehumanized as a mentally disabled woman in a patriarchal society, her shift into monstrous form marks a continuum rather than a rupture. She deterritorializes and reterritorializes the line between human and non-human, emerging as a true posthuman monster: a cyborg-like fusion of woman and animal. While Aijaz Ahmad (1992: 148) reads her as a misogynistic trope—the virgin-turned-vampire—Sufiya is better understood as an agent of regenerative violence. Her acts of brutal vengeance against patriarchal oppression in Karachi reclaim the monstrous as a tool of posthuman resistance, performing corrective justice that exceeds identity politics. Rushdie's posthuman monsters do not reflect the technological optimism of transhumanist discourse. Instead, they challenge both the techno-utopianism of the Global North and the regressive social structures of the Global South. Figures such as Chamcha and Sufiya extend the politics of migrant and female embodiment by mutating into disruptive presences within urban space. These monstrous walkers transgress the normative rhythms of city life, channelling what Braidotti calls "deviant energies" that destabilize the biopolitical order.

This motif continues in *Fury*, where the masked figures of Akasz Cronos—a cyberpunk reimagining of Frankenstein—roam New York City. These figures create a spectral, alienated metropolis. Yet on the fictional island of Lilliput-Blefuscu, the Cronos myth is repurposed by the Elbee revolutionaries led by Babur to overthrow the Indo-Lilly government. Here, posthuman identity is mobilized for a political end, but the revolution ultimately fails by essentializing identity rather than embracing hybridity. Babur's misreading of the myth, which itself subverts the binary between original and copy, reflects the dangers of collapsing the monstrous into essentialist categories. Rushdie also critiques the posthuman through its instrumentalization in global security discourses. In *Shalimar the Clown*, the eponymous character is transformed from a betrayed husband into a globally surveilled terrorist. His portrayal reveals how posthuman language can be co-opted by imperial narratives to reframe racialized bodies as dehumanized killing machines.

The Western state's treatment of Shalimar echoes the monstrous logic applied to Islamic bodies in the post-9/11 risk society. In this instance, the posthuman monster fails to offer an affirmative politics; instead, it becomes the vector of xenophobic paranoia and racial profiling.

These posthuman monsters do more than unsettle individual subjectivity—they also bleed into the topography of Rushdie's cities. The urban spaces they inhabit mirror their fluid, unstable identities. Cities like Los Angeles, Mecca (Jahilia), Florence, Sikri, Bombay, and Karachi are rendered as amorphous, spectral zones—affective and contested. While scholars such as Edward Soja (1989, 1996) and Fredric Jameson have critiqued cities like Los Angeles as postmodern simulacra devoid of historical depth, Rushdie's vision is more politically charged. His cities resonate with Arjun Appadurai's (1996) notion of global "scapes"—transnational flows that unsettle the binaries of centre and periphery. In Rushdie's novels, then, the city becomes a porous, affective space through which the monstrous walker charts a path of resistance. These posthuman figures do not simply haunt the city—they reconfigure it, destabilizing both urban and humanist boundaries. Walking becomes a monstrous, deviant act: a way of moving through space that defies categorization, challenges surveillance, and enacts the radical potential of hybrid identity in the global metropolis.

Futuristic Mythological City Explored through Walks

In Salman Rushdie's novels, the city often unfolds as a layered and mythic space, explored through the motif of walking. The recurrent appearances of the underground and the garden—two contrasting yet entangled spatial metaphors—map a fantastical urban topography where history, memory, and myth coalesce. These symbolic geographies do not remain static but are animated through walks that traverse and destabilize their boundaries. Rosalind Williams (2008) traces the evolution of spatial imagination from the ancient "vertical" cosmology—comprising earth, heaven, and hell—to the "horizontal" worldview of the Renaissance, shaped by geopolitical expansion. This shift prefigures the spatial logic of globalization, where David Harvey's (1989) concept of time-space compression explains how the acceleration of capital flows has collapsed distances, producing an "instant" urban experience. Doreen Massey (1994) underscores how this entrepreneurial capital flattens local specificity, replacing rich, heterogeneous places with sanitized, corporate zones. Fredric Jameson (1991) sees this as a symptom of postmodernism's "depthlessness"—a surface culture resistant to hermeneutics and rooted in the logic of late capitalism.

Rushdie both critiques and reimagines these spatial paradigms. While he engages the vertical cosmology of heaven, earth, and hell, he subverts its moral binaries. In *The Satanic Verses*, the sacred and the profane are deconstructed through the ironic figuration of Gibreel (the angel) and Saladin (the devil). Paradise is represented not as a transcendent realm but as a garden, while hell appears as an underground—each reimagined as playful, critical spaces that resist sacrosanct moral hierarchies.

These spaces, far from being natural or divine, are "artifactual," in Donna Haraway's (1992) sense—produced through the material-semiotic interplay of human and non-human agencies. The underground and the garden, thus, are neither archaic nor utopian but form complex hybrids within the city, dissolving binary oppositions between urban and non-urban, natural and constructed, sacred and secular. In *The Satanic Verses*, Gibreel Farishta's disorientation in the London Underground—both literal and metaphorical—captures the challenge of categorizing the global city. Vassilena Parashkevova (2012) observes that Gibreel's act of "tropicalizing" London mirrors colonial inversion and critiques the imperial gaze. Following Bhabha, she interprets this spatial reinscription as a postcolonial resistance to the rationalized mapping of urban space, exemplified by Harry Beck's scientific rendering of the Underground. John Clement Ball (2004) concurs, reading Gibreel's panoramic acts not as appropriation but as oppositional cartography.

Rushdie complicates these vertical imaginaries further through symbolic juxtapositions. The underworld of the metro intersects with the spectral haunting of Rekha Merchant, who transforms into Alleluia Cone—the Everest climber—at a moment of psychic collapse, merging hell and heaven into a surreal urban montage. The city becomes a kaleidoscopic verticality where the psychic, historical, and mythic intertwine. This layered cityscape is echoed in *The Ground Beneath Her Feet*, where the myth of Orpheus and Eurydice is reinterpreted. Vina Apsara, the Eurydice figure, is not a passive victim but a commanding queen of the underworld who lures Ormus Cama with her mythic magnetism. The underground reappears here not as Freud's repressed unconscious but as a performative, racialized spectacle. Vina is simulated by Meera, and the "depth" of the underground is commodified on stage, blurring boundaries between myth, music, and mass culture. Rushdie's vision resists the binary logic that sees the underground as degenerate nature. Instead, his depiction resonates with Haraway's "artifactual nature." The underground forces in Rushdie are not the sterile, mechanized hellscapes that Lewis Mumford critiques in *Technics and Civilization* (1934) but dynamic sites where human and non-human agencies co-produce hybrid spatial realities.

In *Shalimar the Clown*, the urban legend of the lizard people of Los Angeles—purported subterranean beings hoarding treasures—is parodied. This myth, based on George Warren Shufelt's 1930s investigations, becomes a racialized metaphor for repressed fears of urban disorder, eventually mirrored in the racial violence Max Ophuls encounters in South Central LA. If the underground figures fear and resistance, the garden in Rushdie's novels signifies memory, myth, and multicultural hybridity. Robert Pogue Harrison (2008) suggests that the garden, though echoing paradise, is inherently historical and postlapsarian—a space of human cultivation and responsibility. Rushdie inverts this idea in *Two Years Eight Months and Twenty-Eight Nights* through his concept of Post-Atheism, where God, like paradise and hell, is a human invention. Rushdie's garden cities are not pastoral utopias but urban, contested, mythic spaces. In this, he critiques Ebenezer Howard's (1996, originally published in 1898) suburban Garden City and Le Corbusier's vertical adaptation. In *Two Years Eight Months*, the apartment complex Bagdad in New York parodies these ideals. It is neither orderly nor arcadian but a chaotic, multicultural microcosm—a dystopic Garden of Eden, scarred by politics and migration.

Gardens in Rushdie's fiction are layered with intertextual and cultural references. From Japanese aesthetics of cultivated memory to Hieronymus Bosch's *The Garden of Earthly Delights*, from Voltaire's *Candide* to the symmetrical Islamic chaharbag, Rushdie's gardens resist singular interpretations. Geronimo's *La Incoerenza*—named after Spinoza's notion of inconsistency—epitomizes this ironic syncretism. The perfection of paradise is deconstructed, especially in the violent destruction of Kashmir's Shalimar Bagh, which once symbolized Mughal harmony. The garden, like the underground, is a space of both memory and myth. In the post-9/11 world, Islamic paradises are reimagined not as symbols of peace but as terrorist incentives. Rushdie counters this with images of gardens as multicultural, manmade spaces—symbolic casualties of religious violence. Technology, far from displacing religious imaginaries, reinforces them in the form of techno-transcendence, as David F. Noble (1997) suggests. In *Two Years Eight Months*, the gardener Geronimo becomes a postmodern Adam—a hybrid myth-maker. He inherits the legacy of Aadam Aziz from *Midnight's Children* and cultivates a fractured, futuristic humanity born of both logic and legend. Walking becomes a central motif in these reimagined garden cities. In *Shalimar the Clown*, the character of Shalimar embodies both the beauty and brutality of Kashmir on the streets of Los Angeles. In *Two Years Eight Months*, walking becomes impossible in post-deluge New York, as citizens float or are crushed by the jinns—symbolizing both global detachment and fundamentalist rootedness. Geronimo, as the hybrid leader, restores the "contested ground beneath their feet," enabling them to walk again. Thus, walking—once a banal act—becomes an allegory of resistance, reconnection, and renewal in the altered spatial politics of Rushdie's mythic cities.

Conclusion

Although the urban walks depicted in Rushdie's novels often precede the fully crystallized global order of the twenty-first century, the consciousness of global discourses—and their limitations—remains deeply embedded in the experiences of his walkers. Through the recurring trope of walking, Rushdie explores the mnemonic and affective production of space as an embodied, participatory act, particularly foregrounding the crises faced by cities and figures from the Global South. These walkers disrupt the hegemonic figure of the autonomous, metropolitan, anthropocentric flâneur. Instead, Rushdie presents posthuman, hybrid bodies whose movements challenge dominant narratives of spatial control and belonging. His cities, constructed through vertical imagery—gardens, undergrounds, thresholds—resist the flattening, instantaneous logic of the horizontal global city produced by late capitalism. Moreover, the walkers and kindred figures in public space do not merely navigate the city; they enact forms of resistance and regeneration. They give shape to an ethical and imaginative geography—virtual, fluid, and mobile— that opens up possibilities for alternative spatial imaginaries. In this way, walking becomes a subversive and world-making act in Rushdie's fiction, one that intuitively engages with, and profoundly challenges, the spatial assumptions of the contemporary global urban condition.

7
CONCLUSION

This book delves deeply into the portrayal of cities in Salman Rushdie's novels, offering a critical exploration of how Rushdie's work challenges prevailing metropolitan discourses surrounding cities in the context of globalization. By interrogating and critiquing global urban theories, this study recovers the decentralized flows of globalization that existed long before the dominance of European hegemony. Moreover, it contests global urban theories by emphasizing their limitations and omissions, especially when viewed from the lens of the Global South. Through these analyses, this book reveals that the cities in Rushdie's novels are not only important for understanding contemporary global urbanism but also possess the capacity to subvert the stereotypical positioning of cities in the Global North.

This book engages with several global urban theories, drawing on concepts that allow for an understanding of how cities in Rushdie's novels function in ways that break away from conventional notions of the urban. The book uses Soja's (2000) concept of "synekism" to explain the alternative interconnections between cities in Rushdie's works. This concept emphasizes the significance of cities in the Global South and their unique trajectories of development, which are often overshadowed by the dominant urban narratives that privilege the cities of the Global North. The book asserts that Rushdie's novels provide a platform for rediscovering older flows that have been overlooked in previous scholarship. These flows, which predate the rise of the nation-state and modernity, can be recovered by focusing on the cities in Rushdie's novels. These cities span a vast historical range, from the ancient city of Jahilia in *The Satanic Verses* to contemporary global cities like London, New York, and Los Angeles. The cities in Rushdie's novels are

DOI: 10.4324/9781003106180-7

portrayed as idiosyncratic and distinct, offering an alternative framework that is often beyond the reach of conventional methodologies used to study global cities. This methodology typically valorizes a small group of cities in the Global North, often reducing the complexity of the Global South to mere outposts of Western influence.

Shiv Visvanathan's critique of globalization as a uniquely Western phenomenon is significant in this context (2012). As he argues, globalization is not a new phenomenon and Europe was a latecomer to the systems that have been in place for centuries. Writers like Rushdie and Amitav Ghosh, Visvanathan suggests, demonstrate that Europe did not invent globalization, and their works expose the existing, long-standing global systems that predate European dominance. This book affirms Visvanathan's argument by suggesting that globalization in Rushdie's works is not an invention of the West, but rather an ongoing process rooted in the historical and geographical context of the Global South. This view does not merely reflect an academic critique but a deep rethinking of the space that cities, particularly those in the Global South, occupy in the larger narrative of globalization.

Moreover, this book argues that Rushdie's novels provide a more nuanced and complex view of twenty-first century globalization, especially in their representation of cities. In *The Ground Beneath Her Feet*, for instance, the character Rai's photographs of Indochina reflect a critique of US cultural dominance. While the photographs please an American audience, Rai subtly critiques the cultural imperialism embedded in this form of representation. Through this ambiguity, Rushdie offers a sophisticated portrayal of cultural imperialism under US dominance in globalization, which is more critical than his non-fictional political positions might suggest. This critique of imperialistic globalization reveals a deep ambivalence in Rushdie's work, which this book seeks to unravel.

The book continues its exploration of globalization by concentrating on alternative urban forms and modes of resistance in the Global South, particularly from the perspective of migrants. Chapter 3 builds on Doreen Massey's concept of a "global sense of place," using it to analyze place-making in the cities of the Global South. Massey's theory emphasizes that the production of place is not a static or closed process but is instead shaped by dynamic global forces, including migration, transnational networks, and resistance to neoliberal capital. In this chapter, the book uses Rushdie's depiction of land reclamation in Bombay to show how the city is a site of contestation between global capital and local communities. Rushdie's portrayal of Bombay's urban transformation emphasizes how residents and migrants resist these changes, reclaiming urban space and forging a collective sense of place that resists the homogenizing effects of global capitalism and also nativist drive for place-making as a means of asserting the rights of the 'son of the soil.' The concept of a "global sense of place" serves as a corrective to the one-dimensional view of globalization that sees it solely as a force of economic determinism. Instead, this alternative approach to urban space emphasizes the ways in which local communities in the Global South are actively engaged in shaping their own futures, despite the pressures of global forces.

Chapter 4 explores the production of "home" in Rushdie's novels, further developing the idea of resistance to contemporary forms of globalization. The production of home in the urban spaces of the Global South is a vital theme in Rushdie's work, as the dynamics of displacement, diaspora, and migration are central to his literary universe. This chapter engages with the concept of "scale," specifically how Rushdie's novels expose the politics of scale and the process of home-making as a form of resistance. The book contrasts Rushdie's vision of home with dominant ideologies of home-making, which tend to be performative, consumerist, and commodified in the context of contemporary global society. By contrast, Rushdie's depictions of home-making in the Global South are deeply personal, often connected to the memory of place, history, and community. In using Pierre Nora's modified version of *Le Lieux de Mémoire* (the site of memory), the book reaffirms that Rushdie's novels recover the territoriality of memory and belonging, even in the face of global dislocation.

Rushdie's cities also highlight an important critique of the prevailing concept of "home" in the context of diaspora and globalization. While Pierre Nora's framework of memory locates the individual's sense of belonging within national borders, Rushdie's approach to memory, place, and home-making transcends national boundaries. Rushdie's diasporic experience allows him to engage with both local and transnational memories, illustrating how the homes in his novels are not closed, nationalistic spaces but sites of convergence where multiple global networks interact. These homes—embody the resilience of those who live within them, offering an alternative vision of what it means to belong in a globalized world.

Chapter 5 engages with "post-anthropocentric" theories to offer a revisionist reading of Michel de Certeau's concept of walkers. In de Certeau's original formulation, walkers are individuals whose movement through the city offers a form of resistance to the oppressive systems of power that structure urban life. However, Rushdie's portrayal of walkers in his novels extends this idea by emphasizing their relationship to the non-human world, thus reframing their resistance in the context of post-anthropocentric thinking. The walkers in Rushdie's cities are not merely humans moving through the urban landscape; they are actors whose political resistance is closely linked to their connection with the environment, the city, and the non-human other. This chapter focuses on the smallest scale—the body—demonstrating how Rushdie's characters, through their physical presence and movement within the urban space, become active agents in the creation of alternative global spaces.

In all these discussions, this book has engaged with global urban theories in a way that Gayatri Spivak describes as "ab-use." Rather than simply critiquing or "abusing" these theories, the book uses them as a means of "using Enlightenment from below," which reflects the postcolonial project of engaging with dominant knowledge systems from the periphery. This methodology involves a "double bind" in which Rushdie's novels, with their critique of globalization, are simultaneously products of global flows and active agents in contesting those flows. The book does not simply reject global urban theories but challenges them, offering an alternative vision of globalization that is rooted in the lived experiences of the Global South.

By engaging with global urban theories and applying them to the cities of Rushdie's novels, this book provides a revisionist account of the cities in the Global South. Rushdie's cities offer a unique epistemological framework that can inform the study of contemporary urbanism, particularly in the context of the Global South. The book contends that Rushdie's novels contribute to a growing body of scholarship that rethinks the relationship between literature, space, and urbanism while also offering new insights into the politics of place and identity in a globalized world.

Rushdie's novels are not only literary texts but also vital sources for understanding the social, political, and cultural dynamics of the Global South. By providing a detailed analysis of the cities in his works, this book contributes to the ongoing conversation about the future of cities in a globalized world. The cities in Rushdie's novels—complicated, contested, and full of contradictions—continue to serve as a rich site of resistance and reimagination, offering hope for those who seek to challenge the imperialistic and capitalist forces shaping the contemporary urban landscape. Through these cities, Rushdie's novels reaffirm the power of literature to illuminate the complexities of the global urban condition, providing valuable insights for scholars, activists, and citizens alike. In this way, Rushdie's cities will continue to inspire critical engagement with the challenges facing cities in the Global South, ensuring that they remain central to the discourse on globalization and urban space.

REFERENCES

Abu-Lughod, Janet L. *Before European Hegemony: The World System A.D. 1250–1350*. Oxford University Press, 1989.

Afshari, Reza. "Ali Mazrui or Salman Rushdie: The Satanic Verses and Islamist Politics." *Alternatives*, vol. 16, no. 1, 1991, pp. 107–114.

Ahmad, Aijaz. "Salman Rushdie's Shame: Postmodern Migrancy and the Representation of Women." *In Theory: Classes, Nations, Literatures*, Verso, 1992, pp. 123–158.

Aji, Aron R. "'All Names Mean Something': Salman Rushdie's 'Haroun' and the Legacy of Islam." *Contemporary Literature*, vol. 36, no. 1, 1995, pp. 103–129. *JSTOR*. https://doi.org/10.2307/1208956.

Al-Azm, Sadik J. "The Importance of Being Earnest about Salman Rushdie." *Reading Rushdie: Perspectives on the Fiction of Salman Rushdie*, edited by D. M. Fletcher, Rodopi, 1994, pp. 255–292.

Alter, Robert. "Midnight's Children and Tristram Shandy." *Rushdie's Midnight's Children: A Book of Readings*, edited by Meenakshi Mukherjee, Pencraft International, 1999, pp. 112–115.

Anderson, Benedict. *Imagined Communities: Reflections on the Origin and Spread of Nationalism*. Revised Ed., Verso, 1983.

Appadurai, Arjun. *Modernity at Large: Cultural Dimensions of Globalization*. University of Minnesota Press, 1996.

Appadurai, Arjun. "Spectral Housing and Urban Cleansing: Notes on Millennial Mumbai." *Public Culture*, vol. 12, no. 3, 2000, pp. 627–651.

Appadurai, Arjun. "Cosmopolitanism from Below: Some Ethical Lessons from the Slums of Mumbai." The Salon, Johannesburg Workshop in Theory and Criticism (JWTC), vol. 4, 2011.

Aravamudan, Srinivas. "'Being God's Postman Is No Fun, Yaar': Salman Rushdie's The Satanic Verses." *Diacritics*, vol. 19, no. 2, 1989, pp. 3–20.

Ashcroft, Bill. *Post-Colonial Transformation*. Routledge, 2001.

Ashcroft, Bill. "Transnation and the Postcolonial City." *Australian Humanities Review*, vol. 62, 2017, pp. 46–64.

Assmann, Aleida, and Sebastian Conrad. *Memory in a Global Age: Discourses, Practices and Trajectories*. Macmillan, 2010.

Bachelard, Gaston. *The Poetics of Space.* Translated by Maria Jolas, Beacon Press, 1969.

Ball, John Clement. *Imagining London: Postcolonial Fiction and the Transnational Metropolis.* University of Toronto Press, 2004.

Bardolph, Jacqueline. "Language is Courage." *Reading Rushdie: Perspectives on the Fiction of Salman Rushdie,* edited by D. M. Fletcher, Rodopi, 1994, pp. 209–220.

Batty, Nancy E. "The Art of Suspense: Rushdie's 1001 (mid-) Nights." *Rushdie's Midnight's Children: A Book of Readings,* edited by Meenakshi Mukherjee, Pencraft International, 1999, pp. 95–111.

Benjamin, Walter. *Charles Baudelaire: A Lyric Poet in the Era of High Capitalism.* Translated by Harry Zohn, Verso, 1997.

Bhabha, Homi K. "The World and the Home." *Social Text,* no. 31/32, 1992, pp. 141–153. *JSTOR,* https://doi.org/10.2307/466222.

Bhabha, Homi K. *The Location of Culture.* Routledge, 1994.

Bhabha, Homi K. The Right to Narrate. Harvard Design Magazine no.38, 2014.

Bharucha, Rustom. "Rushdie's Whale." *Reading Rushdie: Perspectives on the Fiction of Salman Rushdie,* edited by D. M. Fletcher, Rodopi, 1994, pp. 159–172.

Birch, David. "Postmodernist Chutneys." *Textual Practice,* vol. 5, no. 1, 1991, pp. 1–7. https://doi.org/10.1080/09502369108582100.

Blunt Alison, and Cheryl McEwan, editors. *Postcolonial Geographies.* Continuum, 2002.

Blunt, Alison, and Robyn M. Dowling. *Home.* Routledge, 2006.

Booker, M. Keith. "Beauty and the Beast: Dualism as Despotism in the Fiction of Salman Rushdie." *ELH,* vol. 57, no. 4, 1990, pp. 977–997. *JSTOR,* https://doi .org/10.2307/2873093.

Braidotti, Rosi. *The Posthuman.* Polity Press, 2013.

Brennan, Timothy. *Salman Rushdie and the Third World: Myths of the Nation.* Macmillan, 1989.

Brenner, Neil. *New State Spaces: Urban Governance and the Rescaling of Statehood.* Oxford University Press, 2004.

Brenner, Neil, and Roger Keil. "From Global Cities to Globalized Urbanization." *The City Reader,* edited by Richard T. LeGates and Frederic Stout. Routledge, 2014, pp. 89–97.

Burgess, Ernest W. "The Growth of the City: An Introduction to a Research Project." *The City Reader,* edited by Richard T. LeGates and Frederic Stout. London and New York, Routledge, 1996, pp. 89–97.

Castells, Manuel. "The Reconstruction of the Social Meaning in the Spaces of Flow." *The Informational City: Information Technology, Economic Restructuring, and the Urban Regional Process.* Blackwell, 1989, pp. 493–498.

Cesari, Chiara De, and Ann Rigney, editors. *Transnational Memory: Circulation, Articulation, Scale.* Walter de Gruyter, 2014.

Chambers, Claire, and Graham Huggan. "Reevaluating the Postcolonial City: Production, Reconstruction, Representation." *Interventions: International Journal of Postcolonial Studies,* vol. 17, no. 6, 2015, pp. 783–788.

Chambers, Claire. "'The Heart, Stomach and Backbone of Pakistan': Lahore in Novels by Bapsi Sidhwa and Mohsin Hamid." *South Asian Diaspora,* vol. 6, no. 2, 2014, pp. 141–159.

rjee, Partha. "Colonialism, Nationalism, and Colonialized Women: The Contest in India." *American Ethnologist,* vol. 16, no. 4, 1989, pp. 622–633.

Childe, Vere Gordon. *Man Makes Himself: An Authoritative History of the Rise of Civilization and of the Means by Which Man Has Achieved Mastery of His Environment.* Watts, 1956.

Cohen, Jeffrey Jerome. "Monster Culture (Seven Theses)." Monster Theory: Reading Culture, edited by Jeffrey Jerome Cohen, University of Minnesota Press, 1996, pp. 3–25

Connerton, Paul. *How Societies Remember*. Cambridge University Press, 1989.

Cook, Rufus. "Place and Displacement in Salman Rushdie's Work." *World Literature Today*, vol. 68, no. 1, 1994, pp. 23–28. JSTOR, https://doi.org/10.2307/40149840.

Cronin, Richard. "The Indian English Novel: *Kim* and *Midnight's Children*." *Rushdie's Midnight's Children: A Book of Readings*, edited by Meenakshi Mukherjee, Pencraft International, 1999, pp. 134–148.

Cundy, Catherine. "Rushdie's Women." *Wasafiri*, vol. 9, no. 18, 1993, pp. 13–17.

Cundy, Catherine. "Through Childhood's Window: *Haroun and the Sea of Stories*." *Reading Rushdie: Perspectives on the Fiction of Salman Rushdie*, edited by D. M. Fletcher, Rodopi, 1994, pp. 335–342.

Davis, Mike. *City of Quartz: Excavating the Future in Los Angeles*. Verso, 1990.

Davis, Mike. *Planet of Slums*. Verso, 2007.

Dawson, Ashley, and Brent Hayes Edwards. "Introduction: Global Cities of the South." *Social Text*, vol. 22, no. 4, 2004, pp. 1–7.

Dayal, Samir. "The Liminalities of Nation and Gender: Salman Rushdie's 'Shame.'" *The Journal of the Midwest Modern Language Association*, vol. 31, no. 2, 1998, pp. 39–62. JSTOR, https://doi.org/10.2307/1315090.

De Certeau, Michel. "Walking in the City." *The Practice of Everyday Life*. Translated by Steven Rendall, University of California Press, 1984, pp. 91–110.

Deleuze, Gilles. *A Thousand Plateaus: Capitalism and Schizophrenia*. Translated by Brian Massumi, University of Minnesota Press, 1987.

Deszcz, Justyna. "Salman Rushdie's Attempt at a Feminist Fairytale Reconfiguration in Shame." *Folklore*, vol. 115, no. 1, 2004, pp. 27–44.

Dirlik, Arif. "Rethinking Colonialism: Globalization, Postcolonialism, and the Nation." *Interventions: International Journal of Postcolonial Studies*, vol. 4, no. 3, 2002, pp. 428–448.

During, Simon. "Postcolonialism and Globalisation: A Dialectical Relation After All?." *Postcolonial Studies: Culture, Politics, Economy*, vol. 1, no. 1, 1998, pp. 31–47.

Durix, Jean-Pierre. "'The Gardener of Stories': Salman Rushdie's Haroun and the Sea of Stories." *The Journal of Commonwealth Literature*, vol. 28, no. 1, 1993, pp. 114–122. https://doi.org/10.1177/002198949302800109.

Dutt, Nargis, performer. *Mother India*. Mehboob Productions, 1957.

Erll, Astrid. "Travelling Memory." *Parallax*, vol. 17, no. 4, 2011, –18.

Fernandez-Armesto, Felipe. *Pathfinders: A Global History of Exploration*. Oxford University Press, 2006.

Fletcher, D. M. "Introduction: The Politics of Salman Rushdie's Fiction." *Reading Rushdie: Perspectives on the Fiction of Salman Rushdie*, edited by D. M. Fletcher, Rodopi, 1994, pp. 1–22.

Foucault, Michel. "Of Other Spaces." *Diacritics*, vol. 16, no. 1, 1986, pp. 22–27.

Frank, Søren. *Migration and Literature: Günter Grass, Milan Kundera, Salman Rushdie, and Jan Kjærstad*. Palgrave Macmillan, 2008.

Frank, Søren. *Salman Rushdie: A Deleuzian Reading*. Museum Tusculanum Press University of Copenhagen, 2011.

Gane, Gillian. "Migrancy, the Cosmopolitan Intellectual, and the Global City in The Satanic Verses." *MFS Modern Fiction Studies*, vol. 48, no. 1, 2002, pp. 18–49.

Gikandi, Simon. "Globalization and the Claims of Postcoloniality." *The South Atlantic Quarterly*, vol. 100, no. 3, 2001, pp. 627–658.

Gregg, Melissa, and Gregory J. Seigworth GJ. *The Affect Theory Reader.* Duke University Press, 2010.

Gregory, Derek. *Geographical Imaginations.* Blackwell, 1994.

Gregory, Derek. *The Colonial Present.* Blackwell, 2004.

Guha, Ranajit, editor. *Subaltern Studies,* Vol. 1. Oxford University Press, 1982.

Györke, Ágnes. "Rushdie and Globalization." *Salman Rushdie in Context,* edited by Florian Stadtler, Literature in Context Series, Cambridge University Press, 2023, pp. 182–192.

Hage, Ghassan. "Migration, Food, Memory and Home-building." *Memory: Histories, Theories, Debates,* edited by Susannah Radstone and Bill Schwarz, Fordham University Press, 2010, pp. 416–427.

Haraway, Donna J. "A Manifesto for Cyborgs: Science, Technology, and Socialist Feminism for the 1980s." *Socialist Review,* vol. 15, no. 2, 1985, pp. 65–107.

Haraway, Donna. "The Promises of Monsters: A Regenerative Politics for Inappropriate/d Others." *Cultural Studies,* edited by Lawrence Grossberg et al., Routledge, 1992.

Haraway, Donna. *When Species Meet (Posthumanities).* University of Minnesota Press, 2007.

Harrison, Robert Pogue. *Gardens: An Essay on Human Condition.* University of Chicago Press, 2008.

Harrison, Robert Pogue. "A Cyborg Manifesto (1985)." *Cultural Theory: An Anthology,* edited by Imre Szeman and Timothy Kaposy, Wiley, 2010, pp. 454–471.

Harvey, David. "From Space to Place and Back Again: Reflections on the Condition of Postmodernity." *Mapping the Futures,* edited by Jon Bird et al., Routledge, 1993.

Harvey, David. *The Condition of Postmodernity: An Enquiry in to the Origins of Cultural Change.* Blackwell Publishers, 1989.

Harvey, David. "The Right to the City." *International Journal of Urban and Regional Research,* vol. 27, 2003, pp. 939–941.

Hayden, Dolores. "What Would a Non-sexist City be like? Speculations on Housing, Urban Design, and Human Work." *Signs: Journal of Women in Culture and Society,* vol. 5, no. 3, 1980, pp. 170–187.

Heidegger, Martin. *Poetry, Language, Thought.* Translated by Albert Hofstadter, Harper Colophon Books, 1971.

Held, David, and Anthony G. McGrew, editors. *The Global Transformations Reader: An Introduction to the Globalization Debate.* Polity Press, 2000.

Herbert, Caroline. "Spectrality and Secularism in Bombay Fiction: Salman Rushdie's *The Moor's Last Sigh* and Vikram Chandra's *Sacred Games.*" *Textual Practice,* vol. 26, no. 5, 2012, pp. 941–971.

Hosain, Attia. *Sunlight on a Broken Column.* Penguin, 1961.

Howard, Ebenezer. "'Author's Introduction' and 'The Town-Country Magnet.'" *The City Reader,* edited by Richard T. LeGates and Frederic Stout, Routledge, 1996, pp. 345–353.

Huggan, Graham. *The Postcolonial Exotic: Marketing the Margins.* Routledge, 2001.

Hutcheon, Linda. *A Poetics of Postmodernism: History, Theory, Fiction.* Routledge, 1988.

Jacobs, Jane M. *Edge of Empire: Postcolonialism and the City.* Routledge, 1996.

Jacobs, Jane M. "The Uses of Sidewalks: Safety." *The City Reader,* edited by Richard T. LeGates and Frederic Stout, Routledge, 1996, pp. 103–108.

Jacobs, Jane M. *The Economy of Cities.* Random House, 1969.

Jameson, Frederic. "Third World Literature in the Era of Multinational Capitalism." *Social Text*, vol. 15 (Autumn), 1986, pp. 65–88.

Jameson, Frederic. *Postmodernism, or, the Cultural Logic of Late Capitalism*. Duke University Press, 1991.

Jennings, Justin. *Globalizations and the Ancient World*. Cambridge University Press, 2012.

Joyce, James. *Ulysses*. Egoist Press, 1922.

Jussawalla, Feroza. "Rushdie's 'Dastan–e-Dilruba': 'The Satanic Verses' as Rushdie's love letter to Islam." *Diacritics*, vol. 26, no. 1, 1996, pp. 50–73.

Kapur, Shekhar. *Mr. India*. Narsimha Enterprises, 1987.

Khan, Sabir. "The Reciprocal Framing of Self and Place in Émigré Autobiographies." *Memory and Architecture*, edited by Eleni Bastea. University of New Mexico Press, 2004, pp. 117–139.

Khanna, Stuti. "Art and the City: Salman Rushdie and His Artists." *Ariel*, vol .37, no. 4, 2006, pp. 21–43.

Khanna, Stuti. "Language and the Postcolonial City: The Case of Salman Rushdie." *The Journal of Commonwealth Literature*, vol. 46, no. 3, 2011, pp. 397–414.

Khanna, Stuti. "Revisiting the City in Rushdie's Fiction." *Salman Rushdie in Context*, edited by Florian Stadtler, Literature in Context Series, Cambridge University Press, 2023, pp. 159–169.

Kortenaar, Neil ten. "Midnight's Children and the Allegory of History." *Rushdie's Midnight's Children: A Book of Readings*, edited by Meenakshi Mukherjee, Pencraft International, 1999, pp. 28–48.

Kortenaar, Neil ten. *Self, Nation, Text in Salman Rushdie's "Midnight's Children."* McGill-Queen's University Press, 2004. *JSTOR*, http://www.jstor.org/stable/j .ctt80rjz.

Latour, Bruno. *Reassembling the Social: An Introduction to Actor-Network Theory*. Oxford University Press, 2005.

Lefebvre, Henri. *Critique of Everyday Life Volume III: From Modernity to Modernism*. Translated by Gregory Elliott, Verso, 2008.

Lefebvre, Henri. *The Production of Space*. Translated by Donald Nicholson-Smith, Blackwell, 1991.

Lefebvre, Henri-. *Writings on Cities*. Edited by Eleonore Kofman and Elizabeth Lebas, Blackwell, 1996.

Lefebvre, Henri. *The Urban Revolution*. Translated by Robert Bononno, University of Minnesota Press, 2003.

Lefebvre, Henri. *Rhythmanalysis: Space, Time and Everyday Life*. Translated by Stuart Elden and Gerald Moore, Continuum, 2004.

LeGates, Richard T., and Frederic Stout, editors. *The City Reader*. Routledge, 1996.

Loughry Treasa De. "Salman Rushdie and World-Historical Capitalism." *Salman Rushdie in Context*, edited by Florian Stadtler, Literature in Context Series, Cambridge University Press, 2023, pp. 264–277.

Massey, Doreen. "A Global Sense of Place." *Space, Place and Gender*, Polity Press, 1994, pp. 146–156.

Massey, Doreen. *For Space*. Sage, 2005.

Mazrui, Ali A. "Moral dilemmas of 'The Satanic Verses.'" *The Black Scholar*, vol. 20, no. 2, 1989, pp. 19–32.

McLeod, John. *Postcolonial London: Rewriting the Metropolis*. Routledge, 2004.

Mendes, Ana Christina. *Salman Rushdie in the Cultural Market Place*. Ashgate, 2013.

Merivale, Patricia. "Saleem fathered by Oskar: Intertexual strategies in Midnight's Children and The Tin Drum." *Rushdie's Midnight's Children: A Book of*

Readings, edited by Meenakshi Mukherjee, Pencraft International, 1999, pp. 116–133.

Mignolo, Walter. "The Many Faces of Cosmo-Polis: Border Thinking and Critical Cosmopolitanism." *Public Culture*, vol. 12, no. 3, 2000, pp. 721–748.

Mishra, Vijay. "Rushdie and Bollywood Cinema." *The Cambridge Companion to Salman Rushdie*, edited by Abdulrazak Gurnah,Cambridge University Press, 2007, pp. 11–28.

Mishra, Vijay. "Salman Rushdie, Aesthetics and Bollywood Popular Culture." *The Journal of Commonwealth Literature*, vol. 113, no. 1, 2012, pp. 112–128.

Mishra, Vijay. *Salman Rushdie and the Genesis of Secrecy*. Bloomsbury Academic, 2020.

Mondal, Anshuman A. *Islam and Controversy: The Politics of Free Speech After Rushdie*. Palgrave Macmillan, 2014.

Mufti, Aamir. "Reading the Rushdie Affair: An Essay on Islam and Politics." *Social Text*, no. 29, 1991, pp. 95–116. *JSTOR*, https://doi.org/10.2307/466301.

Mukherjee, Meenakshi. "Politics and Children's Literature: A Reading of Haroun and the Sea of Stories." *Ariel*, vol. 29, no. 1, 1998, pp. 163–177.

Mumford, Lewis. *Technics and Civilization*. Harcourt, Brace & Company, Inc, 1934.

Nair, Rukmini B. "History as gossip in Midnight's Children." *Rushdie's Midnight's Children: A Book of Readings*, edited by Meenakshi Mukherjee, Pencraft International, 1999, pp. 49–68.

Natarajan, Nalini. "Woman, Nation and Narration in Midnight's Children." *Rushdie's Midnight's Children: A Book of Readings*, edited by Meenakshi Mukherjee, Pencraft International, 1999, pp. 165–181.

Needham, Anurandha D. "The Politics of Post-Colonial Identity in Salman Rushdie." *The Massachusetts Review*, vol. 29, no. 4, 1988, pp. 609–624.

Negri, Antonio, and Michael Hardt. *Empire*. Harvard University Press, 2000.

Noble, David F. *The Religion of Technology: The Divinity of Man and the Spirit of Invention*. Alfred A. Knopf, 1997.

Nora, Pierre. "Between Memory and History: Les lieux de mémoire." *Representations, Special Issue: Memory and Counter-Memory*, vol. 26, 1989, pp. 7–24.

O'Sullivan, Simon. "The Aesthetics of Affect: Thinking Art Beyond Representation." *Angelaki: Journal of Theoretical Humanities*, vol. 6, no. 3, 2001, pp. 125–135.

Parameswaran, Uma. "Autobiography as History: Saleem Sinai and India in Rushdie's *Midnight's Children*." *Toronto South Asian Review*, vol. 1, no. 2, 1982, pp. 52–60.

Parameswaran, Uma. "Handcuffed to History: Salman Rushdie's Art." *Ariel*, vol. 14, no. 4, 1983, pp. 34–45.

Parashkevova, Vassilena. "'Turn Your Watch Upside Down in Bombay and You See the Time in London': Catoptrics Urban Configurations in Salman Rushdie's *The Satanic Verses*." *The Journal of Commonwealth Literature*, vol. 42, no. 3, 2007, pp. 5–24.

Parashkevova, Vassilena. *Salman Rushdie's Cities: Reconfigurational Politics and the Contemporary Urban Imagination*. Continuum, 2012.

Pipes, Daniel. *The Rushdie Affair: The Novel, the Ayatollah, and the West*. Birch Lane, 1990.

Pirbhai, Mariam. "The Paradox of Globalization as an 'Untotalizable Totality' in Salman Rushdie's The Ground Beneath Her Feet." *International Fiction Review*, vol. 28, no. 1/2, 2001, pp. 54–66. http://journals.hil.unb.ca/index.php/IFR/article/view/7691/8748. Accessed 21 April 2013.

Pollock, Griselda. "Modernity and Spaces of Femininity." *Vision and Difference: Femininity, Feminism and Histories of Art,* Routledge, 1988, pp. 50–90.

Pollock, Sheldon. "Cosmopolitan and Vernacular in History." *Public Culture*, vol. 12, no. 3, 2000, pp. 591–625.

Prakash, Gyan. "Writing Post-orientalist Histories of the Third World: Perspective from Indian Historiography." *Comparative Study in Society and History*, vol. 32, no. 2, 1990, pp. 383–408.

Prakash, Gyan. *Mumbai Fables*. Harper Collins, 2011.

Pratt, Mary Louise. *Imperial Eyes: Studies in Travel Writing and Transculturation*. Routledge, 1992.

Radstone, Sussanah. "What Place is this? Transcultural Memory and the Location of Memory Studies." *Parallax*, vol. 17, no. 4, 2011, pp. 109–123.

Ranasinha, Ruvani. "The Fatwa and its Aftermath." *The Cambridge Companion to Salman Rushdie*, edited by Abdulrazak Gurnah, Cambridge University Press, 2007, pp. 11–28.

Reder, Michael R. *Conversations with Salman Rushdie*. University of Mississippi Press, 2000.

Robertson, Roland. *Globalization: Social Theory and Global Culture*. Sage, 1992.

Robinson, Jennifer. *Ordinary Cities: Between Modernity and Development*. Routledge, 2013.

Rothberg, Michael. *Multidirectional Memory: Remembering the Holocaust in the Age of Decolonization*. Stanford University Press, 2009.

Roy, Anindya, and Aihwa Ong, editors. *Worlding Cities: Asian Experiments and the Art of Being Global*. Wiley-Blackwell, 2009.

Roy, Anjali Gera. "Adarsh Nagar Diyaan Gallaan: At Home in a Resettlement Colony." *Interpreting Homes in South Asian Literature*, edited by Malashri Lal and Sukrita Paul Kumar, Pearson Longman, 2007, pp. 16–43.

Rushdie, Salman. *Midnight's Children*. Jonathan Cape, 1981.

Rushdie, Salman. *Shame*. Jonathan Cape, 1983.

Rushdie, Salman. *The Satanic Verses*. Viking, 1988.

Rushdie, Salman. *Imaginary Homelands: Essays and Criticism from 1981–1991*. Granta Books, 1991.

Rushdie, Salman. *The Moor's Last Sigh*. Random House, 1995.

Rushdie, Salman. *The Ground Beneath Her Feet*. Jonathan Cape, 1999.

Rushdie, Salman. *Fury*. Jonathan Cape, 2001.

Rushdie, Salman. *Shalimar the Clown*. Jonathan Cape, 2005.

Rushdie, Salman. *The Enchantress of Florence*. Random House, 2008.

Rushdie, Salman. *Two Years Eight Months and Twenty-Eight Nights*. Jonathan Cape, 2015.

Rushdie, Salman. *The Golden House*. Jonathan Cape, 2017.

Rushdie, Salman. *Quichotte*. Jonathan Cape, 2019.

Rushdie, Salman. *Victory City*. Random House, 2023.

Said, Edward W. *Orientalism*. Penguin, 1978.

Said, Edward W. "The Satanic Verses and Democratic Freedoms." *The Black Scholar*, vol. 20, no. 2, 1989, pp. 17–18.

Said, Edward W. *Culture and Imperialism*. Vintage Books, 1993.

Said, Edward W. *Reflections on Exile and Other Essays*. Harvard University Press, 2000.

Sankar, Dhee. "The 'War of the Worlds': Salman Rushdie from Postcolonial to Posthuman Apocalypse." *Journal of Postcolonial Writing*, November 2024, pp. 1–16. https://doi.org/10.1080/17449855.2024.2420718.

Sassen, Saskia. "Cities: A Window into Larger and Smaller Worlds." *European Educational Research Journal*, vol. 11, no. 1, 2012, pp. 1–10.

Sassen, Saskia. *The Global City: New York, London, Tokyo*. Princeton University Press, 1991.

Schultheis, Alexandra. *Regenerative Fictions: Postcolonialism, Psychoanalysis and the Nation as Family*. Palgrave Macmillan, 2004.

Simawe, Saadi A. "Rushdie's 'The Satanic Verses' and Heretical Literature in Islam." *The Iowa Review*, vol. 20, no. 1, 1990, pp. 185–198. *JSTOR*, http://www.jstor.org/stable/20152976. Accessed 9 April 2025.

Soja, Edward. *Postmodern Geographies: The Reassertion of Space in Critical Social Theory*. Verso Press, 1989.

Soja, Edward. *Thirdspace: Journeys to Los Angeles and Other Real-and-Imagined Places*. Basil Blackwell, 1996.

Soja, Edward. *Postmetropolis: Critical Studies of Cities and Regions*. Basil Blackwell, 2000.

Soja Edward, "Putting Cities First: Remapping the Origins of Urbanism" A Companion to the City, edited by Gray Bridge and Sophie Watson, Wiley, pp 26-34, 2003.

ak, Gayatri C. "Can the Subaltern Speak?" *Marxism and the Interpretations of Culture*, edited by Cary Nelson and Lawrence Grossberg, Macmillan Education, 1988, 271–316.

Spivak, Gayatri C. "Reading the Satanic Verses." *Public Culture*, vol. 2, no. 1, 1989, pp. 79–99.

Spivak, Gayatri C. *An Aesthetic Education in the Era of Globalization*. Harvard University Press, 2013.

Stadtler, Florian. "Terror, Globalization and the Individual in Salman Rushdie's Shalimar the Clown." *Journal of Postcolonial Writing*, vol. 45, no. 2, 2009, pp. 191–199.

Suleri, Sara. *Meatless Days*. University of Chicago Press, 1989.

Suleri, Sara. "Contraband Histories: Salman Rushdie and the Embodiment of Blasphemy." *Reading Rushdie: Perspectives on the Fiction of Salman Rushdie*, edited by D. M. Fletcher, Rodopi, 1994, pp. 221–236.

Syed, Mujeebuddin. "Midnight's Children and its Indian Con-texts." *Rushdie's Midnight's Children: A Book of Readings*, edited by Meenakshi Mukherjee, Pencraft International, 1999, pp. 149–164.

Teverson, Andrew. "Fairy Tale Politics: Free Speech and Multiculturalism in 'Haroun and the Sea of Stories.'" *Twentieth Century Literature*, vol. 47, no. 4, 2001, pp. 444–466.

Teverson, Andrew. "The Number of Magic Alternatives: Salman Rushdie's 1001 Gothic Nights." *Empire and the Gothic*, edited by Andrew Smith and William Hughes, Palgrave Macmillan, 2003.

Teverson, Andrew, editors. *Postcolonial Spaces: The Politics of Place in Contemporary Culture*. Palgrave Macmilan, 2011.

Thiara, Nicole W. "Enabling Spaces and the Architecture of Hybridity in Salman Rushdie's The Enchantress of Florence." *The Journal of Commonwealth Literature*, vol. 46, no. 3, 2011, pp. 415– 431.

Thrift, Nigel. "Driving in the City." *Theory, Culture and Society*, vol. 21, no. 4–5, 2004, pp. 41–59.

Tilly, Charles. "Cities, States, and Trust Networks: Chapter 1 of *Cities and States in World History*." *Contention and Trust in Cities and States*, edited by Michael Hanagan and Chris Tilly, Springer, Dordrecht, 2011. https://doi.org/10.1007/978-94-007-0756-6_1.

Trivedi, Harish. "Salman the Funtoosh: Magic Bilingualism in Midnight's Children." *Rushdie's Midnight's Children: A Book of Readings*, edited by Meenakshi Mukherjee, Pencraft International, 1999, pp. 69–94.

Tuan, Yi-Fu. *Topophilia: A Study of Environmental Perceptions, Attitudes and Values*. Prentice Hall, 1974.

Upstone, Sara. "Domesticity in Magical-Realist Postcolonial Fiction: Reversals of Representation in Salman Rushdie's 'Midnight's Children.'" *Frontiers: A Journal of Women Studies*, vol. 28, no. 1/2, 2007, pp. 260–284. JSTOR, http://www.jstor.org/stable/40071959.

Upstone, Sara. *Spatial Politics in the Postcolonial Novel*. Ashgate, 2009.

Varma, Rashmi. "Provincializing the Global City: From Bombay to Mumbai." *Social Text*, vol. 22, no. 4, 2004, pp. 65–89.

Varma, Rashmi. *The Postcolonial City and its Subjects: London, Nairobi, Bombay*. Routledge, 2012.

Visvanathan, Shiv. "For a New Epistemology of the South." *630 Shiv Visvanathan, for a New Epistemology of the South*, 2012. www.india–seminar.com/2012/630/630_shiv_visvanathan.htm. Accessed 4 June 2016.

Watt, Ian. *The Rise of the Novel: Studies in Defoe Richardson and Fielding*. University of California Press, 1957.

Williams, Rosalind. *Notes on the Underground*. MIT Press, 2008.

Wilson, Keith. "Midnight's Children and Reader Responsibility." *Reading Rushdie: Perspectives on the Fiction of Salman Rushdie*, edited by D. M. Fletcher, Rodopi, 1994, pp. 55–68.

Wolff, Janet. "The Invisible Flâneuse: Women and the Literature of Modernity." *Theory, Culture & Society*, vol. 2, no. 3, 1985, pp. 37–46.

INDEX